SYNCHRONICITY

By the Author

Truly Wanted

Truly Enough

Truly Home

Synchronicity

Visit us at www.boldstrokesbooks.com

SYNCHRONICITY

by

J.J. Hale

2024

SYNCHRONICITY

ISBN 13: 978-1-63679-677-2

THIS TRADE PAPERBACK ORIGINAL IS PUBLISHED BY
BOLD STROKES BOOKS, INC.
P.O. BOX 249
VALLEY FALLS, NY 12185

FIRST EDITION: OCTOBER 2024

CREDITS
EDITOR: JENNY HARMON
PRODUCTION DESIGN: STACIA SEAMAN
COVER DESIGN BY TAMMY SEIDICK

Acknowledgments

To my family, who put up with my last-minute deadline panics no matter how long I give myself to get stuff done. I will never get things done at a comfortable pace, and I'm thankful you still put up with my self-induced spirals.

To everyone who had a part in nurturing my love of dance from a very young age, and those who took a chance on me when I dipped my toes into teaching. It was a beautiful five years of my life seeing the joy it brought to the kids who were learning to love it, too. More importantly, to those who reminded me it's okay to love something without monetizing it—that was the most important lesson to learn. The experience it gave me helped shape this story and reminded me that I can dance anytime, and anywhere I want, even if it may bring some funny looks!

To everyone who worked on this story in any form, most especially my editor, who continuously makes sure I understand the whys that make me a better writer.

To all of the readers who have given me so much motivation over the past few years. Your love for my words and characters means more than I can explain to anyone outside of my head. It's the best form of external motivation to get more words out and stories created.

To everyone who needs a reminder of the joy dancing can bring, when life doesn't allow a lot of time for it. Make time to dance, even if it's alone in your kitchen to the music in your head.

CHAPTER ONE

Haley Tyne's stomach flipped with anticipation as she placed a sweaty palm around the chipped, gold-painted handle before her. She took a deep breath before pushing the door open and was immediately greeted with the cacophony of chatter from the already crowded bar. It was to be expected on a Friday night at Willow's, the designated sapphic spot in the city. Or so Haley assumed, considering she had never been to a queer bar before.

Haley's heart began to pick up speed as she glanced back from the still-ajar door and out to the footpath that she had passed a hundred times before but had never dared to step off her well-trodden path. Until tonight. She took a moment to adjust to the sensory overload of the noise and took a few deep breaths.

Come on, Haley. You can do this.

The silent pep talk propelled Haley's legs across the threshold as the door shut behind her. She had built herself up for this moment so much that it was almost a letdown that the bar looked like any other. Dimly lit, noisy, and smelling of stale beer and cigarettes despite the fact that nobody smoked indoors anymore. Somehow, the scent still lingered in tightly packed pubs.

As Haley made her way toward the bar and looked around at the patrons, her stomach began to flutter. Willow's might look like any other bar she had been in on the surface, but the clientele was subtly different. She wasn't sure exactly what she had been expecting, but it was everything and nothing like her imagination had conjured.

Some patrons fit into the stereotypes she had in her head, but an overwhelming majority didn't. Regardless of the fact that people wore a wide variety of different clothes and hairstyles, most were undoubtedly queer. Haley was sure she had never been around so many women who were so comfortable with other women.

As Haley passed couples kissing or talking close together, trading soft caresses of arms or thighs, she tried to pull her eyes away so as not to stare. She got to the bar and found a spot in the throng of people clamouring for their next drink as her pounding heart continued its faster-than-usual pace.

Haley's eyes darted in all directions to take in more of the crowd around her as she waited to place an order. It wasn't as busy as she had initially thought upon entering. The crowd thinned out as people took their drinks and headed toward tables or booths at the back, or some toward the large dance floor. Her eyes locked onto the dance floor, and Haley feared they would seem comically bulged were someone to glance at her.

She was used to dance floors in nightclubs, at least the few she had attended in college. Clubbing wasn't Haley's thing, or hadn't been when the floor was filled with sweaty guys groping and grinding against her while her skin crawled. The college club scene had always been touch first, ask questions later, and nobody did a thing about it.

Watching the writhing bodies on the busy dance floor tonight told a different story. Everyone involved in the sensual movements seemed to be an enthusiastic participant, and Haley couldn't blame them. Her body flushed watching them dance. She couldn't imagine how it would react to being in the midst of it.

"You plan on ordering or just gawking a little longer?"

It took Haley a minute to understand that the question was directed at her. Her cheeks heated as she stared back at the bartender who looked at her with questioning eyes. The annoyance grew on the bartender's face as Haley opened and closed her mouth, trying to remember what she was supposed to order or why she was even there.

What was I thinking? I'm not ready for this.

It was all too much. Haley tried to form at least an apology before she turned on her tail and dashed out of there. Before she could get the words out, though, a strong hand was placed upon her shoulder.

"She'll have the same as me, T. Keep the change."

Haley turned her head to see who the silky smooth voice belonged to and met the eyes of the most beautiful person she had ever seen in real life. The stranger had deep slate grey eyes and full lips that were raised in an amused smile.

"You're new here."

The stranger framed it as a statement rather than a question, and Haley's face heated even more.

"That obvious?"

Haley was proud of herself for forming coherent words, even if there were only two of them so far.

"You've got the whole deer in the headlights thing going for you. I'm Cal, by the way."

Cal put out her hand and Haley shook it, much to her new companion's amusement. That's when Haley noticed the bartender had returned with their drinks, which Cal had been reaching for. Haley closed her eyes for a moment and wondered if her face would ever return to its natural colour. She could only hope that the low lighting shielded some of her shame.

"Thanks, I can pay you back for this," she said as she held up the glass before taking a sip.

"Wait, is this water?" Haley asked in confusion as Cal chuckled beside her.

"Yep. I don't make a habit of getting women drunk without at least knowing what they like to drink first. I'm a gentlewoman like that. But I find an ice-cold glass of water does wonders to clear your mind. You looked in need of something to shock your system back into action."

The water was ice cold, and Cal wasn't wrong. Haley took another gulp from the glass, and as the cold liquid slipped back her throat, her hands stopped shaking.

"Good choice," Haley said.

"I make a lot of those," Cal replied with a wink that sent the butterflies in Haley's stomach into overdrive.

Haley stood at the bar, sipping the refreshing drink and wondering what to do next. She was still tempted to leave. She had done what she promised herself she would do, which was enter the bar and prove to herself that it wasn't such a scary place to be. She hadn't thought far beyond that.

As her eyes moved back in Cal's direction, Haley knew that the last part was a lie. In the darkness of her room, as she lay in bed over the past few weeks, she had thought about other things that could occur after venturing inside.

Cal was wearing a sleek navy pair of khakis that were paired with a fitted grey shirt that almost matched her eyes. There was a black belt buckled at her waist that looked like it was more for show than functional. It was worth the added touch. Haley moved her gaze toward the jet-black hair that was slicked back in a bun before her eyes fell to those lips again. The deep natural colour of her lips were a contrast to her warm ivory skin.

Those lips would appear as stars of the show in her dreams for the foreseeable, she was sure of it. Haley moved her gaze up to meet Cal's and was sure the appreciation wasn't hidden in her eyes. Surprisingly, at that moment, Haley didn't care. She was openly appreciating a woman for the first time, and that woman was looking at her with something that hinted at intrigue, if not interest.

"Would you like a real drink now?" Cal asked.

A part of Haley was desperate to tell Cal the thoughts running through her brain of exactly what she would like. The slight quirk of Cal's eyebrow made Haley think her face was doing it for her.

"Sure. I'll have whatever you're having."

Haley was grateful for the steadiness of her voice. As she kept her eyes trained on Cal, she noticed that the butterflies that still fluttered weren't nerves. In fact, the anxiety she had had since before she entered the bar had dissipated almost entirely. In its wake was a longing Haley hadn't experienced in a long time. A raw hunger that left little room for concern.

"You just had what I'm having. But I can get you an alcoholic drink if you'd prefer. What do you want?"

You.

If Haley thought the words loud enough, she hoped that maybe they'd make their way into Cal's head. She wasn't quite brave enough to ask for that yet. Rejection wasn't something she dealt with well at the best of times, but from a woman like Cal, it would be even more of a blow than usual. Hell, a few short minutes ago she didn't even know this woman's name. But with the vibrations of the loud music pulsing through her body and the heat of the bodies bustling around them, Haley wanted to know everything about her.

Cal leaned in closer, and Haley's heart flipped.

Did it actually work? Was she about to kiss me?

Haley closed her eyes in anticipation before a soft breath tickled her ear as Cal whispered loud enough to be heard above the music.

"Do you want to dance instead?"

Haley opened her eyes as Cal pulled back and held out a hand. One intended for Haley to take this time. Haley slipped her smaller hand into Cal's as she led the way to the dance floor already packed with bodies. They made their way between groups and couples until Cal stopped and pulled Haley's hand to her waist. Haley gulped and hoped her body would take over because her mind was in no place to give directions.

Luckily for her, dancing was as natural to Haley's body as breathing, and she began to sway to the rhythm of the sensuous song. Cal moved to the same beat as she placed a featherlight touch against the small of Haley's back. Cal gently urged her closer, more a suggestion than a command. It was a suggestion Haley's body willingly accepted.

Haley tuned into the softness of Cal's shirt beneath her fingertips on the curve of Cal's hip. She dug her fingers in a little tighter as they moved closer, and Cal nudged Haley's arm up to wrap around her shoulder. They were almost flush against each other now. Cal was taller than Haley's five foot four, so she had to arch her neck to look up as Cal stared down.

Their eyes stayed locked as the music wound its way around them like an invisible string. It pressed their bodies together in a way that was almost synchronized. Cal's strong hand turned gentle as she caressed the sliver of skin above the small of Haley's back where the material of her top had ridden up. The action sent shocks through Haley's body, and she bit back a whimper as fire flashed in Cal's eyes.

Cal leaned down again, and this time Haley anticipated the soft whispers that were as intimate as any kiss she had ever experienced.

"Is this okay?"

Cal's request for reassurance left Haley speechless for a moment as lust as she had never known coursed through her veins. At Haley's nod, Cal tipped her chin up to make their eyes meet.

"I want to hear it from you, please."

The sincerity in Cal's gaze as it searched Haley's almost brought tears to her eyes. Why did this affect her so damn much? Cal stilled her movements which had Haley's mouth opening to get them back in any way possible.

"Yes. Yes, it's okay, I promise."

Haley's steady voice seemed to soothe Cal's concerns as her soft fingertips resumed their path along Haley's spine and they pressed closer together again.

It's just a dance. We're just dancing.

Haley tried to remind herself of the facts as her body throbbed in places that dancing never usually called for. She was used to her limbs being heavy from the exertion of a dance, but not the aching between her legs that intensified with every beat.

She silently begged those lips to meet hers, and by the fire burning in Cal's eyes, her wordless pleas weren't going unheard. Haley searched her face for a reason, any reason why Cal wasn't answering the unspoken request. It wasn't a lack of desire because the darkening of Cal's eyes was unmistakably fuelled by lust.

Haley flicked her tongue out across her bottom lip and Cal's eyes followed the movement. Cal's mouth parted before she pulled her own bottom lip between her teeth. Haley would bet anything on the fact that Cal was stifling a moan. She couldn't have made herself any clearer if she had written it on her forehead and yet Cal made no move to put them both out of their misery.

Fuck this, Haley Jane Tyne. You are a strong, independent woman and you can take what you want instead of silently begging.

Haley willed her second pep talk of the night to have as good a result as the first. She prepared herself to reach up on her tiptoes and press her lips against Cal's in a way she already knew would shatter any misgivings she had about her attraction to women. Before she had the chance, the music switched to a more upbeat pop song and Cal slowed both of their movements.

They stood staring at one another for what seemed like a lifetime but was only a few beats of the far too peppy for her mood song.

Kiss me, goddammit.

Haley had lost her nerve, pep talk be damned, and she was back to the silent pleading as Cal's gaze seemed to take in every inch of her face. Then, so suddenly Haley didn't see it coming, everything stopped. Cal's fingers were no longer on her skin and her body already missed the heat of hers as she took a step back.

"Have a good night."

The words were spoken in a rushed, stilted voice that held no hint of the confident, smooth tone she had used until now. Cal turned and disappeared into the crowd. Haley glanced around at the people still singing and dancing as if the whole world hadn't shifted on its axis. The damn pop song blared as a loud reminder that barely a minute had passed since Haley had been sure she would end this night finally in the arms of a woman. Instead, she was alone in a sea of happy couples, wondering what the hell had just happened.

Happy fucking birthday to me.

Chapter Two

Cal O'Shea stepped out of the noisy pub and was surprised to find it was brighter outside than in. It was still barely ten, and with summer in full swing, the sky was more of a deep blue in contrast to the darkness of the dimly lit establishment where she worked. She had finished in Willow's an hour ago, having covered the early shift, and should have been well home by now.

Cal stopped to take a breath and went to pull out her phone and check in at home before grabbing a bus that would take her on the twenty-minute journey there.

"You didn't even ask my name."

The softly whispered words were loud on the empty street as Cal turned to face the reason for her delayed departure. Her companion for the past hour somehow managed to look even more beautiful than before, despite the harsh floodlight outside the bar.

"You're right, I didn't," Cal replied. She left off the part about how that had been purposeful, but her words implied as much. Cal didn't do names. She generally didn't do dances with innocent-looking newbies either, but here they were. Cal recalled the not-so-innocent way the woman's body pressed against hers, and her eyes dropped to the kissable lips that had been obviously begging for her. *Looks can be deceiving.*

"Usually, the ditch them without a name or number thing happens after the sex, though, right? Or is that different with women too? I admit I'm not a pro at one-night stands, but I definitely didn't think it included just dancing."

Cal's mouth dropped open and she couldn't help but laugh. The feisty look written all over her companion's face was a far cry from the nervous wreck that had stopped her on her way to the door after her shift and had her veering toward the bar instead.

"You have a point there, newbie," Cal said as she slid her phone back into her pocket. She would check in in a few more minutes, Cal told herself. She was already late, a few more minutes wouldn't change much.

"Newbie?"

"Well, we already established that you're quite clearly new here. And I don't know your name, so it seemed fitting."

Cal shifted closer to Haley as a group moved between them to enter the bar. They both moved to the side in unison and found themselves face to face at the side of the bar, where the dark but familiar alley led to the direction of her bus stop.

"You could just ask, you know."

The words drew Cal's eyes down to the bow-shaped lips that kept capturing her attention.

"Or you could skip that part and kiss me the way you're thinking about right now."

Cal's own surprise was mirrored on the face in front of her as if the words were spoken with no permission from their owner. Cal stared into the depths of the blue eyes staring back at her as a longing stronger than any she had experienced in a long time wrapped itself around her gut.

"You're trouble, you know that?"

Cal whispered the words as they moved even closer together until their fingers brushed. The electricity that moved through her body at the contact had Cal wondering what would happen without the barriers of their clothing, or public setting for that matter.

"I'll take trouble over newbie. Sounds much cooler."

The grin that tugged at those beautiful lips had Cal's stomach twisting with lust. She needed to get home. She needed to stay away from tempting blondes with bodies that moulded too perfectly with her own. She needed to do anything except the thing she wanted to do the most.

"What are you afraid of?"

You.

Cal kept the reply to herself and tried her best to affix her cool and calm persona back in place. She had managed to keep her mask intact for so long, she rarely considered it a persona anymore, until tonight. Until she had been on the dance floor pressed against the first person in years who made her want to forget everything, and everyone, and lose herself in their explosive chemistry for the night. And therein lay the problem. Cal had responsibilities she couldn't afford to forget, even for the beautiful temptress before her.

"I need to get going. My bus is due soon and I still need to get to the stop." Cal pointed down the alley as she dodged the question.

"Your bus stop is down the scary dark alley that seems to have no end?"

Cal grinned at the clear scepticism on her companion's face.

"It has an end, you just have to turn to the right after the second dumpster back there to get out the gate. Which is technically private property, but I work here, so I do this often. Most people walk around the footpath, but that adds on at least ten minutes."

"Ten minutes that could save your life. I don't feel good sending you down a dark alley alone. I feel like this is one of those movies where I'll be a suspect in your murder as the last person to see you alive."

Cal laughed and shook her head at the statement.

"You're funny. Would you like me to write a note to say you didn't do it before I head down there? Got any paper?"

Cal wagged her eyebrows as she turned to walk backward, and the woman reached out to hold Cal's arm and stop her in her tracks.

"I'm serious. You can't go down there alone. I can walk that way with you and call a cab from the other side."

Cal bit her lip to stop the grin from forming.

"What? You're more afraid of being alone with me down a dark alley than by yourself?"

The salacious tone dripping from the words sent shivers down Cal's spine that were undoubtedly not from fear.

"I'm just wondering how exactly you'll protect me from the apparent murderer awaiting us."

Cal was all too aware of the hand still placed on her arm as her self-appointed protector moved closer to her until the darkness of the alley surrounded them both.

"I'll have you know, I'm stronger than I look."

The heat that radiated between them multiplied tenfold in the semi-privacy of their spot that was shielded from the street.

"Looks can be deceiving," Cal mumbled, smiling to herself at the echo of her earlier thought.

"I'm going to say this once because I'm pretty sure I'm bordering on desperate, but if I walk away from here tonight knowing I didn't make myself abundantly clear, I know I'll regret it. And I don't like to have regrets."

Cal knew what was about to be said because it had been clear from the moment their eyes met that this was where they both wanted the night to lead. This gorgeous woman was about to ask to be kissed, again, and Cal couldn't let that happen. Nobody who was willing to put themselves out on a limb like this when the attraction was clearly mutual deserved to feel anything less than absolutely desirable.

Cal placed a finger over the woman's lips and turned them to press her back lightly against the wall of the pub. A soft "oh" slipped out around her finger, and Cal moved her hand down to trace a soft finger along the exposed skin of her neck.

"I really do need to go. Which has nothing to do with me not wanting to be here with you because trust me, I do." Cal dropped her gaze to the now silent mouth in front of her and back up to the blue eyes pooled with lust before continuing. "You might not believe my words, but I hope this proves it."

With that, Cal leaned her head in and finally pressed their lips together softly. The slow, gentle kiss soon made way for a hunger with the stroke of their tongues melding together.

Shit. Trouble indeed.

Cal had no doubt from the way they danced together that

kissing this woman would be good. But there were no words to accurately describe the sensations rushing through Cal's body as her hands pressed against the exposed skin of the woman's waist. Arms wrapped around her to press them closer together, and Cal groaned at the pressure already building inside her. A pressure she absolutely could not relieve in the alley attached to her workplace.

Cal pulled her lips back slowly as the sound of their laboured breathing filled the air around them. Her fingertips continued to stroke lightly against the skin beneath them as a quiet whimper escaped the lips she had just been kissing. If Cal didn't leave now, she would be kissing them again until they were both aching in places that already throbbed.

"I really need to go," Cal whispered as she reluctantly pulled back until their skin no longer met at all.

A soft nod was her only response and she turned to go, willing her feet to carry her on the familiar route.

"Wait."

Cal stopped moving but didn't turn around. If she did, Cal feared she would never make it home.

"I'm not sure that my accompanying you farther into this alley is a good idea right now because I doubt either of us will make it home anytime soon. Can you at least take my number to let me know you got home safe? If that's all you ever use it for, that's okay. No expectations."

Cal wrestled with herself for a moment. Taking a number from someone she made out with wasn't a precedent she usually liked to set. But then again, nothing about their encounter so far was usual. If this woman said she had no expectations, Cal owed it to her to take her at her word. Cal pulled her phone from her pocket and unlocked it before turning to hand it over.

As a smile lit up the woman's face, Cal thought that maybe, just maybe, she could use the number for more than a welfare update. It had been so long since Cal had explored anything solely for herself. Anything outside of the realm of responsibilities she had undertaken. Responsibilities she knew needed to come first. But maybe it was time to find room to tiptoe back into a part of life just for her. If the beautiful smile aimed her way wasn't enough motivation to consider it, nothing would be.

Cal took her phone back and walked backward again for a moment as a sheepish wave from her companion brought another smile to her face. A thought occurred to her then, as she realized she still hadn't asked her name. She checked the time, which showed that the last bus was almost due, and turned to hurry toward it before bringing up her contacts. She searched for the new entry as she made her way safely to the stop right before the bus pulled away. The word keyed into the name field of the number made her laugh, even if it provided no answer to the mystery.

Trouble.

CHAPTER THREE

Y ou're home late."
	Haley was startled by her mom's voice as she walked through the front door of her childhood home.

"Geez, Mom, you scared me. What were you doing, peeking out the window waiting for my return?"

Her mom shook her head as she continued walking down the entrance hall toward the living room.

"I've got far more important things to do with my time, darling. I just got up to boil the kettle for a fresh cup of tea while the ads are on. Why don't you make us both some and you can tell me what has you out gallivanting at all hours on the next break."

"It's not even midnight yet. I'm sure that doesn't fall under *all hours*," Haley replied, but her mom was already rushing back into the living room at the first notes of the theme tune to her beloved soap opera. Haley couldn't imagine sitting through commercial breaks only to watch fifteen minutes of a TV program anymore. Those days were long gone for everyone but her mother, who insisted on watching regular TV channels through a regular satellite dish no matter who said what.

You're always in too much of a rush, Haley, her mom would say, *life isn't about how quickly you can live it.*

Haley poured them both tea and brought it into the living room. She sat on the small, worn-in one-seater chair that she had claimed as hers long before she remembered doing so. Her mom sat across from her, eyes focused on the dramatic scenes playing out on the screen. There was no pausing the show to chat in this house. Not where Irene Tyne was concerned. Haley would wait until the commercial break and endure three minutes of interrogation before the show came back on. Then she could disappear to her room to relive the night and all the glorious details she would not be sharing with her mother.

"So, where have you been? Because I know for sure it wasn't Orlaith who put that dreamy smile on your face."

Haley chuckled, both loving and hating how well her mom knew her. Orlaith was Haley's best friend and the person she spent most of her free time with, so it was the obvious go-to excuse. But clearly, that wasn't going to fly tonight.

"I do not have a dreamy smile," Haley huffed.

The protestation was pointless apart from buying her a little time to gather her thoughts. Because explaining where she had been would lead to questions about why she had gone there. Which would lead to questions about her sexuality. Questions she had yet to fully answer for herself, never mind anybody else.

"We're on a clock here, Hales. What's with the secrecy all of a sudden?"

Her mom kept her voice light, but lines of concern formed between her brows. They didn't do secrets and they never had. At least, not that her mom was aware of. Growing up, her mom had always given her the space to figure things out and been there to talk it through when needed. They had talked openly about pretty much everything throughout Haley's life, everything but this.

"Haley Jane, what's going on?"

Haley blinked back the sudden and unexpected tears that had begun to well and cursed her mother's eagle eyes.

"Mom, I…"

The first notes of the theme tune came back on, and she glanced toward the screen as if it was her salvation. This could wait, right? It wasn't a big deal. It didn't need to be. Except, the screen went black, and she looked back to see her mom setting down the remote control.

"It was only a rerun anyway. Now, use those words I know you have in there and tell me what's going on."

Haley sniffed and was thankful that her mom didn't try to comfort her. She had learned a long time ago that physical comfort wasn't helpful to her and only caused her to feel panicked and overwhelmed. It wasn't that she was against hugs or physical touch as a whole, but it wasn't a comfort at times where she was already struggling to find her words.

Her mom sat with her as she gathered her thoughts, and Haley was overcome with a rush of gratitude. For the woman who allowed Haley to be who she was and feel how she felt in the way that worked best for her. Her mom had only ever shown her acceptance, so why would it be any different now?

"Mom, I think I'm bisexual."

There, it was out. Haley had spoken the words aloud that she'd had rolling around her head now for months. Her mom sat for a moment, expression unchanged, before she nodded softly.

"Yeah, that makes sense. I thought you might be a lesbian, but you were really into that second guy, what was his name again? So bisexual makes sense."

Haley blinked once, then again, processing the words her mom had spoken.

"Ruairí. That was his name. You were head over heels for him for a while until he turned out to be a dick."

"Mom!" Haley slapped a hand over her mouth before bursting into laughter.

"Well, am I wrong? Maybe you'll have better taste in women than you've had in men. A mother can dream."

Haley tried to control the laughter that stemmed from both shock and relief as her mom beckoned her over to the couch. Haley moved into her mom's arms, and warmth spread through her at the gentle stroking of her hair. Her mom always knew when Haley needed space, but equally when she needed to be held.

"You weren't afraid to tell me, were you?" her mom asked softly.

"No, not exactly. I think I was more afraid to tell myself. And telling you meant it was real, and I wasn't ready for that. Until now."

"That makes sense. So what changed tonight?"

Cal.

The name swam around Haley's head as scenes from the evening flashed before her eyes. She had been so concerned about labelling herself with something that might not even be true and having to retract it later. Which, in itself, was a silly notion. As if someone came and tattooed *bisexual* across her forehead once she announced it and she had to go get it removed if she were wrong. Haley had a love/hate relationship with labels in general, a constant worry about being defined incorrectly.

But in the same way that the label of her ADHD had only helped her understand herself better, so did bisexual. Any concerns about being wrong had evaporated the moment Cal's body pressed against hers. She was bisexual, and for now, that label fit right.

"I met someone." Haley whispered the words gently after the silence stretched too long.

"Told you it was a dreamy smile," her mom said. She squeezed Haley's shoulder before Haley moved to sit back.

"Yes, yes, you were right," Haley replied. She stuck out her tongue in jest, and her mom chuckled.

"Very mature, Hales. I see your newfound sense of self hasn't enhanced your maturity."

Haley pulled a cushion into her lap and tugged at the frayed edges.

"Tell me about her," her mom said as she sipped her tea.

"She's tall, dark hair, eyes that look like they can see into your soul. But she's not a relationship person."

"That's never stopped you before. Although as I said, I had hoped you'd have better taste in women."

Haley couldn't argue with that. She had a habit of ending up with guys who never wanted anything more than casual. A fact that most of them neglected to say up front. Haley wasn't good at half measures, and when she had feelings for someone, she was all in. When it became clear that they weren't, it left Haley wondering what was wrong with her. What was it about her that made people not want anything serious, even after a year together, as evidenced by her relationship with Ruairí. At least Cal had the up front part going for her.

"I'm not getting involved with her, don't worry. But we kissed, and it was amazing, and I have no doubts after that that I like women."

Haley's cheeks heated as the memories of how amazing kissing Cal was flushed through her body.

"So, she was like your bisexual awakening then?"

Haley wrinkled her nose at the word awakening and saw the grin on her mom's face.

"Nah, I'm pretty sure the first awakening was that dance teacher I had when I was six. It just went back to sleep again, clearly."

Her mom laughed and shook her head as Haley grinned.

"Awakening, reawakening, whatever you want to call it. That's an important role to play in someone's life. I hope she was deserving of it."

I hope so too, Haley thought as a yawn escaped her.

"Come on, time to turn in. We have a busy day ahead of us tomorrow."

Haley groaned as she set her alarm for seven hours' time and headed to bed. Saturdays were always busy at the dance studio her mom owned and ran, where Haley was training to teach. She would have back-to-back classes from morning until late afternoon followed by rehearsal for the summer recital they put on yearly. Haley changed into her cosy pyjamas and crawled under the covers. She checked her phone to see no new messages. She hoped Cal had gotten home safe, and tried to remind herself that Cal didn't owe her anything. Even so much as a quick text message. Part of Haley wished she had taken Cal's number instead, but it would be a lot worse had she messaged first and gotten no response.

Part of understanding how ADHD affected her brain had come with learning about rejection sensitive dysphoria and the way it impacted Haley every single day. Knowing what RSD was, and that it made any real or perceived rejection that much worse for her, didn't always help lessen the impact. Despite years of therapy to understand that other people's commitment issues weren't a reflection of her, RSD was not something to be reasoned with. Rejection hit her hard and deep and made even the idea of feeling that way again terrifying. That meant that Haley needed to be more mindful of the situations she put herself in, and the expectations she set.

If Cal hadn't messaged by morning, Haley would take it for what it was. Cal wasn't interested in anything, casual or otherwise, and that didn't detract from the night or Haley's experience. It had been a sensual, thrilling evening that she would likely always remember.

Awakening.

As cringy as it sounded coming from her mom, it fit. Haley was more awake, more alive than she could ever remember being, and this night was one she would never forget. A confidence had grown in her outside the bar, and the way Cal had responded to it made Haley want more.

Not more of Cal, although that was something she wouldn't turn down, but more of herself. More of the confident, in charge person she had become once the anxiety of the evening had ebbed away. For too long, Haley had been going with the flow of whatever life brought. Whatever guy decided to pay her attention, or whatever friend wanted her time, or whatever job her mom threw her way. It hit her now that she had been a passenger in her own life, allowing others to steer her in whatever direction suited. Fear of failure, of rejection, or more accurately of her reaction to rejection, had made Haley play it too safe for too long.

It was time Haley took back the wheel. She wasn't unhappy with the direction of her life, but she wanted it to be a purposeful one. Haley was in control of her destiny, and tonight, she really believed it. Haley didn't need Cal, or anyone else, to be a driving force in embracing her sexuality. No matter how good it was to have Cal's lips pressed against hers. Even if it was Cal's face that appeared in her mind as Haley's fingers made their way beneath the waistband of her pyjama pants to finish what Cal had started mere hours before.

No, Haley didn't need Cal. But she sure as hell wanted her.

CHAPTER FOUR

Cal couldn't wipe the smile off her face as she pressed down the handle of her weathered front door and stepped through the threshold. The scent of her unexpected companion's perfume still clung to her shirt. A reminder of how close they had gotten that night. She took out her phone, pulled up the contact, and smiled again at the name attached to the number.

The house was quiet, which wasn't unusual given the time. Her mom and sister were early to bed most nights, and Cal was far later than usual. She pulled up a message and tried to think of a flirty way to say she got home safely as she flicked on the light switch to their small living room. Her phone tumbled out of her hands, and the soft carpet muffled the sound of the thud as Cal took in the scene before her.

It only took seconds to process what was happening, because unfortunately it wasn't the first time she had stumbled upon a similar situation. Memories began to flash through her mind as she fixated on her mother's limp body lying on the couch with empty blister packs strewn upon the coffee table beside her.

Not again.

The sound of a soft sniff pulled Cal back to the present and her eyes landed on her eleven-year-old sister, Maeve, curled in a tight ball in the small spot between the couch and the wall. It was her favourite hiding place and a comforting escape when the world was too much.

"Maeve, did you call 999?"

Cal kept her tone as even and quiet as she could, not wanting to startle her already overwhelmed sister. She bent to pick the phone up from where it had fallen and called the emergency services as Maeve sat still with her eyes trained ahead and her lips sealed.

"It's my mom. She's overdosed on tablets. We need help."

Cal's voice cracked as she rattled off the address and approached her mom to check her pulse at the operator's request. It was there. She was alive.

For now, the voice in her head chimed in, but Cal shut it down quickly. Her mom was alive and likely out of it, if the empty alcohol bottle to her side was any indication. Cal hurried back out to open the front door and leave it on the latch after the operator promised the ambulance wasn't far out. She returned to the room and knelt in front of Maeve, keeping enough distance as to not accidentally touch her, but close enough that her presence was obvious.

"There's going to be some people coming into the house very soon. They'll be helping Mom. They might want to ask you some questions but it's okay if you can't answer. If you want to tell me anything, you can do that, and I'll tell them. But if you want to go to your room and hide while they're here, that's okay too."

Sirens grew closer as Maeve gripped her knees tight against her chest and rocked gently. That was a good sign. It meant Maeve was trying to calm herself.

"They're almost here, Maeve, you okay with being in here?"

A soft nod was the only response Cal got, but it was enough. She pulled down the weighted blanket they kept on the armchair and placed it next to Maeve in case she needed to disappear, and then turned her attention to the sounds of people coming through the door.

"Do you know how much she took?"

One paramedic began trying to rouse her mom as the other came over to talk to Cal.

"No I…I was late. I just got home, and she was like this. I assume the empty packs on the table."

The paramedic's eyes landed on Maeve before coming back to Cal.

"Does she know? Is she okay?"

Cal pondered the question. The paramedic likely meant physically, but no, Maeve wasn't okay. She was an eleven-year-old who had been sitting next to her barely conscious mother for God knows how long because Cal had been late. Because Cal had been out kissing someone instead of here making sure Maeve and her mom were safe.

Again.

"Are you okay?"

The soft press of the paramedic's hand on her shoulder jolted Cal out of her thoughts.

No. I'm not okay. I dropped the ball and now my already traumatized little sister has more trauma to add to the pile. I'm not fucking okay. None of us are.

But of course that's not what she said.

"Yeah, just shocked, I think. Both of us."

The paramedic gave her shoulder a squeeze before moving toward Maeve.

"Wait, don't touch her."

The paramedic gave Cal a quizzical look with a hint of concern as they stopped their movements.

"Sorry, my sister is autistic. She doesn't like to be touched by strangers. She's regulating herself and she'll let me know if she needs anything, but she's okay. Physically, at least."

The paramedic nodded and moved back toward their colleague. The two of them quickly moved Cal's mom to a stretcher with a bag of fluids making their way through the IV already placed in her arm.

"We need to move," the other paramedic said in a hushed voice, but the urgency in the tone was unmistakable. Fear clawed its way up Cal's throat and threatened to make its way out of her mouth in the form of a violent scream, but she clamped it down. Now wasn't the time to lose it. Cal didn't get to fall apart, not when she was so busy trying to keep everyone else together.

Which you're clearly doing a stellar job of.

"What's her name, love?" the paramedic asked while indicating toward her mother.

"Clara," Cal whispered as she hoped the threatening tears wouldn't accompany the word.

"Do you want to come with us?"

The paramedics gave her a sympathetic look as they gathered their supplies and started to make their way to the front door. Cal glanced between her mom's still body on the cold, sterile stretcher and Maeve's small shape outlined beneath her weighted blanket.

"I need to stay with her. I'll follow when I call someone to come over."

Except that was a lie because there wasn't anyone to call. There was nobody else. But the paramedic accepted the answer and disappeared through the door and into the vehicle already primed to go. As the lights from the ambulance faded from view, Cal found herself staring out the window at the darkness left behind.

"Kay…"

The softly spoken word drew Cal's attention and she moved back to sit on the floor in front of Maeve. The moniker only Maeve used for Cal that used to grate on her nerves now tugged at her heart.

"I'm here, May. You're safe."

The first time Cal had ever called her May, Maeve had lit up with glee. *We match, May and Kay,* Maeve had exclaimed before wrapping her arms around Cal's body and clinging to her in the way she seemed to reserve solely for her big sister. An honour Cal had yet to feel worthy of.

"Is Mom dead this time?"

The words broke Cal's heart, none more so than the final two. *This time.* A reminder of the fact that this was more than a one-time thing her sister had to endure. Cal had gotten too complacent. It had been so long since things were bad. She had hoped Maeve would forget about how it was before, but it was obviously as clear in her memory as it was in Cal's.

"No May, she's not dead," Cal said softly.

"But she could die, right, in the ambulance or at the hospital?"

There was no point in giving her sister anything less than the truth. Maeve's brain worked best with the facts, whether they were good or bad. Facts were something she could understand and rationalize far more than platitudes.

"She could. But hopefully I got here in time."

Maeve's grip on her knees loosened and she glanced at Cal.

"You were home late."

It was a statement Maeve made without accusation or anger. Facts. But that didn't stop the guilt laden dagger the words drove through Cal's gut.

"Yes, I was. I'm sorry."

One of the tears that had been threatening to spill broke free and made its way down Cal's cheek. Maeve reached out her hand and swiped it away with her finger before patting Cal's head softly in the way Cal often did for her.

"It's okay. Can we make pizza?"

Cal smiled despite herself and turned her head to mask the tears that followed the first. She hopped up and walked toward the kitchen. She stopped on the way to grab the empty glass bottle to throw in the bin. She was glad that the paramedics had bagged up the blister packs and taken them with them.

"I think that sounds like a good plan, little May. Pizza and then movie in bed, how does that sound?"

Cal set the oven to preheat as the sound of Maeve's footsteps followed her into the room.

"I think that sounds like a good plan, big Kay."

Cal smiled at Maeve's cheeky grin as she slid into a chair at the kitchen table while Cal rummaged through the freezer for their favourite pizza. It was past midnight already, but sleep wouldn't be claiming either of them any time soon. As they sat together and shared a pizza, Cal's thoughts raced with how she would manage being here for Maeve plus being there for her mom in the hospital. It wasn't the first time over the past few years since she'd returned home that Cal wished she could split herself in two.

Cal would call the hospital to check on her mom and let them know she was trying to get there. She would wait until Maeve fell asleep and have the next door neighbour sleep in here with her. She had no doubt Mrs McDonald had seen the ambulance already, and sure enough when she glanced at her phone there was a message from her asking if everything was okay and offering to help. It was seldom Cal ever accepted it because help had a habit of coming wrapped up in pity toward her and judgement aimed at her mother. But needs must.

Maeve wouldn't be happy about it, but hopefully she would sleep through, and Cal could get a taxi to the hospital and be back before Maeve woke in the morning. Cal would load up on caffeine and they could have a movie day tomorrow so her sleep deprivation wouldn't be too bad.

"You can go to the hospital. I can take care of myself."

Maeve spoke the words confidently after evidently reading the dilemma on Cal's face with accuracy. A skill Maeve had mastered far too early on.

"I'm not leaving you here alone. You're eleven," Cal replied.

"I was six the first time I remember being here alone. So I'm five years older now. I even made pizza."

Cal's heart sank at the nonchalant way Maeve spoke about the neglect she had endured while Cal was away at college and oblivious to it. Too wrapped up in her own problems. Problems that, in comparison, were inconsequential when she considered them now. The thought of all the ways it could've gone horribly wrong for her six-year-old sister here alone had already made their way through her mind many times, and now the new information of her operating the oven alone added more terror to the what-ifs.

"I'm sure you did great. But ovens are not for six-year-olds to use alone, and I'm here now."

Maeve rolled her eyes exaggeratedly and Cal chuckled at the action.

"I could read at six, you know. The instructions are right there on the box, it's not that hard. I know how to take care of myself."

You shouldn't have to.

"I know you do. But that's not your job, okay?" Cal said firmly.

"It's not yours either."

The words were spoken softly, and far less confidently than the previous ones Maeve said. Cal reached a hand out to cover Maeve's smaller one on the table.

"It is now, because I want it to be. So stop arguing with me and let me do it. I'll get Mrs McDonald to come over here when I go to the hospital. I know you won't like it but she's not that bad, and I'll make it up to you with even more pizza tomorrow."

Maeve grumbled at the mention of their neighbour but thankfully didn't protest too much as they made their way up to Cal's room. Cal popped a movie on the small screen beside her bed.

"I'm going to pretend to be asleep to avoid her constant questions. So you can turn off the movie."

Cal laughed and tucked Maeve under the covers before stroking her hair softly. As Maeve's eyes fluttered closed, Cal got up from the bed so she could go speak to their neighbour before calling the hospital. She stopped in the doorway to her bedroom and glanced back. She flashed back eleven years to the fourteen-year-old Cal, who resented the new addition to a family Cal already felt like she didn't belong in. A family that had once been just her and her mother disappeared the night Cal set eyes on her mom's positive pregnancy test. It was replaced by two expectant parents of a new bundle of joy who didn't have time for the resentful teenager in their home.

She remembered the anger and hurt at the new perfect baby who demanded the little attention Cal used to get. If she could tell that version of herself how much room that little girl would take up in her heart all these years later, Cal would never have believed it.

"I love you, little May," Cal said as swiped more tears from her cheeks. With eyes still tightly shut, Maeve spoke in the sweet voice that had won Cal's heart.

"I know you do, big Kay."

Chapter Five

Two years later

"C'mere to me, what's this I hear about you ditching me for the summer?"

Haley stifled a laugh as Orlaith, her best friend and the closest thing she had to a sibling, stared her down with a disapproving frown.

"I'm going to volunteer at the summer camp for kids at risk of educational disadvantage. That's hardly ditching you."

Orlaith sighed loudly as she crossed her arms.

"I can't exactly get mad when you're doing good things, but I'm still not happy you'll be gone. How long?"

Haley winced before mumbling, "I'll be back by the end of August."

"*A month?*" Orlaith shrieked, and Haley couldn't help but laugh.

"You act like this is completely out of the blue. I told you about the training I did a few weekends ago to prepare for this. Remember?"

Orlaith was looking over Haley's shoulder, and Haley turned to see what had grabbed her attention.

"I'm sure you'll find ways to occupy yourself in my absence," Haley replied with a grin as the newest object of Orlaith's affection walked through the studio doors. Orlaith's cheeks pinked immediately as she refocused on Haley. Indie was the newest addition to their studio, and Orlaith had been drooling over her since the first day she walked through the door. Not that Haley could blame her. Indie was tall and muscular, with tight braids and deep brown skin. Haley envied her sense of style that came from more than just the clothes she wore. Indie was wrapped in a confidence and presence that had more than Orlaith's head turning when she walked into a room.

"Hush," Orlaith said before the cause of her heated face appeared beside them.

"What's going on over here? Is this a private conversation or can anyone join?"

Haley smiled widely at Indie, who was the studio's first and only hip-hop instructor. Haley taught modern dance at the studio her mother had founded when she was young, and Orlaith taught contemporary dance. With the studio's reputation plus its sliding scale fees and scholarship programs, classes were packed six days a week.

"I actually need to go set up for the teen group, they'll be here any minute. So I'll leave you both to it."

Haley aimed a conspiratorial smile at Orlaith as she backed away and left her and Indie alone. Orlaith looked like a deer in the headlights as Haley laughed and made her way to the biggest room in the studio.

As Haley got the room prepared, she popped on some music and smiled at the sounds drifting from the speakers attached to the walls of the mirrored room. There was nothing quite like the few moments before a class began. The large, mostly empty room filled with nothing but music waiting to be put to good use.

Haley moved her feet in rhythm to the familiar song as the melody wrapped its way around her body. She had never been good at sitting still, but luckily dance had always provided her with the excuse she needed to keep her body moving. She moved along the large room and let her body flow to the practiced steps of the choreography that had won first place at last month's regional dance competition.

"You still got it, Miss Tyne."

Haley grinned at the student who was always first through the door for every class she attended.

"I should hope so. I'm only ten years older than you, Branna. Cut it out with the Miss."

Branna grinned and dropped her water bottle at the side before joining Haley in the middle of the floor.

"But it makes you sound more professional, and you need all the help you can get," Branna said with a mischievous smile.

"Oh, you're going to regret that. I think we'll start off our warm-ups with a plank," Haley said.

Branna groaned and stuck out her bottom lip in a pout.

"I'm sorry, I didn't mean it. Anything but that," she pleaded as the door opened and a stream of teenagers walked through.

"Did Branna earn us the plank again?"

Dale, who had been with the studio since he was six, which was almost as long as Branna, shot a withering look their way.

"Yup. Bottles at the sides and everyone drop down. We'll start with a minute."

The resounding grumbles and groans were drowned out as Haley turned up the volume of the music and got to work.

An hour later, as the thoroughly exhausted teenagers gathered their bottles to leave, Branna slinked her way toward Haley.

"You still going to camp this year?" Branna asked with a hopeful look on her face.

"Absolutely. I've got my stuff packed and I'm driving down tomorrow to help set up. You'll be down Sunday, right?"

Branna grinned widely and nodded.

"I can't wait. I made so many friends last year, and they are coming back too. I told them about you, and they can't wait to meet you. They think it's cool that you're, you know, like us."

Haley's heart filled with emotions she couldn't quite place, and she squeezed Branna's arm affectionately. Branna was the reason Haley got the chance to do this, and she was grateful for the opportunity to help. They were looking for someone to coordinate the dance program this year, and as the camp director put it, Branna had raved so much about Haley that they couldn't not reach out to her.

Knowing that there would be a whole host of neurodivergent kids experiencing this for the first time, who often didn't get the chance to participate in classes or camps that weren't set up for them, made Haley well up with emotion. The camp was one of the first of its kind, with a ton of support available and even space for parents to stay if necessary. The aim was to give kids independence and empowerment as much as possible while providing a safe space to make it accessible to all.

Along with the dance program that Haley would oversee, there were programs for art, drama, science, technology, and a smattering of classes in various other areas. Whatever they could get volunteers to run they would be offering over the course of the camp.

"See you Sunday, Miss Tyne."

Branna waved as she headed toward the door, and Haley turned toward the locker room.

"Enough with the Miss," Haley replied to Branna's retreating form.

"So is this where we say our goodbyes, then?"

Haley scoffed at Orlaith's dramatic line as she walked into the locker room to grab her stuff. That had been Haley's last class of the morning, and she had taken the afternoon off to finish packing.

"Don't pretend like we aren't going to text every day. Plus, you'll need to keep me updated with any developments involving a certain someone who makes you swoon."

Haley chuckled at the soft smile that adorned Orlaith's face involuntarily at the mention of Indie.

"A summer without me here playing third wheel might be just what you two need to stop dancing around each other, so to speak."

Haley waggled her eyebrows as Orlaith groaned at the pun and pulled her into a tight hug.

"I'm going to miss your face, Hales. But hey, maybe you'll find someone to do some dancing of your own with at camp."

Haley chuckled as they pulled back, and she slung her backpack over her shoulder.

"It's a dance program, Orls. I should hope so."

Orlaith glared before they began walking toward the studio doors together.

"You know what I mean. I can't wait to hear all about your illicit camp hookups and dirty dancing. Just forgo the unwanted pregnancy part of the story."

"You're hilarious," Haley deadpanned.

"Not like illicit dirty dancing with strangers is a foreign concept to you," Orlaith said. That earned her a death glare as Haley regretted ever telling her about that night.

"Sorry, sorry," Orlaith said with a smile. "But seriously. It's been too long since you've been with anyone. Your last actual relationship was..."

Orlaith trailed off as if trying to remember.

"My last relationship was a perfect example of why it's been so long since."

"Ah yes, Ruairí the dick," Orlaith said as she glanced around to make sure no little ears were nearby.

"You talk to my mother too much. But no, I meant Nate."

"Nate was barely a relationship. That was, what, a few weeks?" Orlaith asked.

"Six months, Orls. You probably don't remember because he made zero effort to get to know anyone in my life. I wasted half a year of my life on someone who, in hindsight, never gave as much as I did to the relationship. He had one foot out the door before it even began, and I ignored the warning signs because I wanted it to work. Ruairí was the same. I'm not good at casual, Orls, and it seems to be all I attract."

Orlaith gave her another hug as they stepped out of the studio.

"You broke up with him three years ago, Haley. You're not the same person you were when you dated either of them. Maybe it's time to give yourself a chance to believe it. Now go enjoy camp and don't miss me too much."

Haley said her goodbyes as she exited the studio to make her way toward the bus stop that would take her home. Her mind flashed back to the aforementioned illicit dance that stood out in her mind.

She could hardly believe that had taken place almost two years ago now. She barely remembered that version of herself. Closeted, terrified, and yet somehow bolder and daring than she had managed to be since.

Grey eyes filled Haley's mind as she sat at the bus stop, and her body heated in the way it had every time Cal popped into her head. Haley had had little more than a brief moment with Cal, and yet she could still fill her thoughts, both waking and sleeping. It was a mystery. In fact, everything about Cal bar her name and stunning beauty was a mystery to Haley.

Cal was most likely wandering around somewhere with no idea of the impact she'd had on Haley's life. She had probably forgotten all about the woman whom she had enraptured with a few sentences and a body that moulded to Haley's like none before or since. A woman whose name Cal didn't even know. It was something Haley had purposefully ensured at the end of the evening in the hope the intrigue would spark at least a message to ask.

The lack of any text message after that night well and truly shut that door, which was probably for the better. Haley had only been coming to terms with her sexuality, and adding a dark haired, captivating beauty into the mix would've surely derailed the path of her own self-discovery. To Cal, Haley was probably one of many captivated women she had shared a dance with. To Haley, Cal was the catalyst to her coming out to her mother, and ultimately her self-acceptance.

Despite being out as bisexual since the night of her first time at Willow's, Haley had yet to return to the establishment. She liked to tell herself that it was due to her ramped up work schedule after she had finished training and taken on a full time role with the studio. But if Haley were to reach inside and pull the truth from the depths of where it hid, it was much more than time that kept her away. Haley no longer feared walking through the door of the place that had seemed so elusive to her before. Now her fear lay in what waited inside.

Haley got on the bus and sat for the short journey home as the memories bombarded her. She pulled her bottom lip between her teeth and applied soft pressure to distract her body from the growing sensation. The truth was, Haley was terrified that she would walk into the bar and those eyes that filled her dreams would be trained on someone else. Or worse, that they would look her way with no recognition in their depths. Haley worried that this proverbial stranger would be just that, and the fantasy she had created in her head would come tumbling down.

At least this camp would be an opportunity to step outside her comfort zone and try something new. Haley had promised herself that fateful night that she would take control of her life and make it purposeful, and the truth was, that promise was yet to be fulfilled. She still lived with her mom. Granted, that was more practical than paying exorbitant rent prices or needing a car to live further out of the city. And she still worked at her mom's studio, which she loved, and was thankful to have a job she genuinely cared about. She still hadn't seriously dated a woman, but she had been focusing on herself and not diving head first into a new relationship until she was ready for that.

But this was what happened anytime Haley considered making a change. She could always find reasons and excuses for why her life was the way it was. She was content, it was easy, she was comfortable. But that's not what your twenties were supposed to be about, right? Haley felt like she had skipped right over the exploration part of her life and gone straight to a routine-driven, comfortable existence. She worried she would wake up in twenty years' time feeling unfulfilled and regretful about the years she spent thinking *comfortable* was the best it could get for her.

A summer camp wasn't much, but it was the most out of routine thing she had done in, well, two years. It was time away from her mom, her friends, and the studio. She would be living in a whole new place for weeks surrounded by people she barely knew, and that terrified and excited her all at once. And who knew, maybe Orlaith was right. Maybe she'd find her own summer fling to push her out of her romance rut and ignite her passion again. Like she had when those strong arms were wrapped around her as her back was pressed against the cold stone wall at the side of the bar. Maybe a summer camp romance was the key to getting the memory of Cal off her mind, and body, once and for all.

Chapter Six

Y ou've got twenty-seven minutes until you need to be in the car with your seatbelt fastened."

Cal rolled her eyes at Maeve and continued to throw clothes into the suitcase on her bed.

"How are you not even packed yet? We're going to be late," Maeve said in an exasperated tone as she walked into Cal's room.

"You just said I've got twenty-seven minutes. Plenty of time."

Cal shot a grin over her shoulder as she closed the suitcase. She held it down and struggled with the zipper as it got jammed in an unruly sleeve poking through the side.

"Twenty-six now. Your clothes are going to be a ball of wrinkles when we get there. I don't even know if they have an iron at this place."

Cal pumped her fist in triumph as she got the zip closed all the way and turned to face Maeve, who was staring at her with a distinct lack of amusement.

"I wouldn't use it if they did. I'll hang them up and they'll be fine. We're hanging out in the woods for the summer. It's not like I need my Sunday best."

Maeve shook her head and turned to go, as if Cal were a lost cause not to be reasoned with.

"Twenty-three," Maeve exclaimed before going back down the stairs to wait impatiently. Her suitcases had been packed for a week already. Everything but her toothbrush, which she promptly rectified after brushing her teeth this morning. Which reminded Cal that she had yet to tackle her toiletries. Those would need to go in her backpack because if she opened that suitcase again it would pop like one of those old school jack-in-the-boxes.

Cal set about dumping her toothbrush and toiletries into a plastic bag to shove into her backpack. She dragged her solitary suitcase down the stairs and placed it beside Maeve's three coordinated cases with a thump. Cal was both awed and amused by Maeve's level of organization at the ripe old age of thirteen. Something Cal clearly still hadn't mastered.

"See, I've still got fifteen minutes to spare, and all I need to do is grab train snacks," Cal said as she turned toward the kitchen.

"Thirteen. And I already packed us a bag of snacks and drinks for the train journey. And Mom made us sandwiches."

Cal groaned internally at the thought of her mom's attempt at a packed lunch and hoped they'd be serving food on the train.

"I sure did. Let's get these bags in the car so we can get on the road before Maeve bounces out of her skin."

Clara bounded down the stairs and grabbed her car keys from the hook beside the door.

They loaded the bags into the boot of the old but reliable car that her mom had purchased second-hand only a few months prior. After Clara got a new job, which was out of the way of the bus route, it made sense to finally give in and get a car, especially considering the salary made the expense worth it. They were still catching up on bills and expenses from the year her mom had been out of work, but Cal was finally starting to see the light at the end of the very dark tunnel they'd been through.

They wound their way through the familiar streets on the short journey to the train station, and Cal looked over at her mom sitting in the driver's seat. The woman confidently driving the car was a far cry from the woman Cal had found passed out on their couch almost two years ago. A scene that still ran through Cal's mind more often than she liked to admit. The night stood out for so many reasons, surprisingly not all of which were horrible. That night had been a catalyst to a change in her mom that Cal had never seen before.

Although Cal feared the backslide that inevitably came every time things got too comfortable, almost two years later it had yet to come.

"You sure you'll be okay here without us? You will visit, right?"

Cal kept her voice low, not wanting to worry Maeve. She needn't have worried as she looked back and saw her sister's trademark noise cancelling headphones firmly in place and the soft head bobbing that indicated music from her phone was the only thing she was listening to.

"Yes, Cal, I can manage for a summer without my two daughters monitoring my every move. I promise."

Cal bit back a quick retort as her mom continued.

"I know you're worried, and I know you have every right to be. But I'm keeping up with my therapy appointments and I've set extra reminders for my medication. Mrs McDonald has invited me over for dinner already and you girls aren't even out of the city yet. Work is going to keep me busy, and I promise I'll visit exactly how we've planned. Focus on enjoying this time, please. You both need it."

Cal tried to believe everything her mom was saying. She knew that her mom believed it. Cal had no doubt her mom's intentions were pure. But intentions didn't always matter when things went wrong and there was nobody there to stop the regression.

"I need it too, Cal. I need to prove to you and myself that things have changed, and I can manage. You can't spend the rest of your life babysitting me, or your sister. You need to focus on your life too."

Cal cleared her throat before replying.

"I'm just a call away if you need me."

Her mom reached out to ruffle Cal's hair as they sat at a red light.

"I know, kiddo. And one day soon, I'll get to say that to you."

"Green light, Mom," Maeve said from the backseat as both Cal and her mom chuckled.

"Yes, boss," Clara replied to an oblivious Maeve, who was still listening to music. She sat up straighter as their mom moved the car forward and turned into the train station set down area. They parked up and got the suitcases from the car to wheel them into the station and buy their tickets from the ticket machine.

"Maeve, why does this say the next train is forty-five minutes from now? You said they were on the hour," Cal groaned.

"Not true. I said they were every hour. You chose to assume I meant on the hour, and if that got us here with less chance of missing it, I wasn't about to correct you," Maeve replied.

Cal's mom snickered behind them as Cal shot Maeve a glare and purchased two train tickets for the next available time. Which was not in fifteen minutes as planned. On the plus side, she would have time to source nicer food while they waited.

"Okay, girls, I need to go so I'm not late for work. You have everything you need?"

Cal turned toward her mom and her heart thumped, another prick of fear lodging its way inside her.

"We do, but if we're missing anything, you can bring it when you visit anyway, right?"

Cal tried to keep her tone casual, but the look on her mom's face told her she failed.

"I'll be there, okay? I promise."

Cal nodded as her mom reached out and squeezed both their hands in a familiar gesture. It was something she had been doing for years. Their mom wasn't much of a hugger, which was fine with Cal considering neither she nor Maeve were either. But this small gesture was her way of providing reassurance and comfort.

"Our train is departing from platform four and there's a bench right there next to it, so we can go wait there," Maeve said, snapping Cal out of her daze as their mom walked out of the station. The sliver of fear refused to budge, but Cal told herself she needed to swallow it down and not let it tarnish any of this experience for Maeve.

"The train isn't taking off for another forty minutes, I'm not sitting on a bench for that long. We'll go get food in the café and see if there's any good magazines for the journey."

Maeve gave Cal a quizzical look and stayed firmly rooted to the spot.

"We have food, Mom packed it. And I've never seen you read a magazine in your life."

"Magazines are reserved for train journeys or waiting rooms, so clearly you haven't been to enough of those with me. And you can eat your sandwich from Mom, but I want real food. If you don't complain then I'll throw in a hot chocolate, and we can go directly to the bench after."

Maeve's face brightened at the mention of hot chocolate, as Cal knew it would. Her weakness.

"Fine. But when you waste money on a magazine to sit with your face in your phone the whole time I'm going to say I told you so."

Cal smiled and slung an arm around Maeve's shoulder as they made their way toward the one and only café on the opposite end of the small station.

"You know I'm too stubborn to prove you right, kiddo. I'm going to devour every word in that magazine just to make my point."

"It's your brain cells on the line, not mine. Those magazines are filled with fake dramatic stories to make people feel better about their own lives."

"Can't argue with that, little May. But it works. I feel almost normal when I read them." Cal laughed as they reached the café.

"You're definitely not normal," Maeve replied with a hint of a smile on her lips. The smile slipped as they reached the café and saw the throng of people queueing inside.

"Hush. You stay here and guard the bags and I'll go get what we need, that okay?" Cal asked.

Relief flooded Maeve's face as she grabbed her headphones to slip them back over her ears and quieten some of the noise of their surroundings. Cal smiled as she glanced back at Maeve before heading to queue up.

Cal thought back to when she had first returned home from college. The difference between the misunderstood, overstimulated child she had found then compared to the teenager who was so capable of regulating herself now was stark. Maeve had skills that

Cal envied when it came to owning, accepting, and regulating her emotions. Better than Cal's current method of burying it down somewhere deep and dark and hoping it never popped up again.

The prick of fear poked at her insides then as a reminder that nowhere was deep or dark enough to keep it all at bay for long. They had all come so far in the past couple of years. Well, Maeve and her mom had at least. Their progress was so clear, so obvious and something Cal was immensely proud of. But lately, Cal had begun to notice how little she herself had progressed in any area of her life.

She was stagnant, in survival mode doing nothing more than trying to make sure they all got through each day and the dangers life held. And even as the obvious dangers had eased, Cal's guard refused to drop. When chaos didn't rule their days, it just felt like the calm before the storm. Cal had spent so long anticipating storms that she had neglected everything else. Mainly herself, and the dreams she used to have.

Cal made her way back out and handed Maeve her hot chocolate, smiling at the excited squeal she got in response. If Maeve's happiness and her mother's safety meant sacrificing some far-fetched dreams, Cal was okay with that. Once things stayed on track a bit longer, Cal could revisit what was left of her own life and rebuild the parts she had lost. That is, if the prickles of fear would dissipate long enough for her to truly believe things were ever going to be okay.

CHAPTER SEVEN

L ast fifteen minutes, gang, let your body loose and just move whatever way feels comfortable." Haley shouted to be heard over the music. She moved to the corner to survey the group and get a sense of their goal for the duration of the camp. This was her favourite part of teaching. Meeting a new class, seeing all the raw potential and the eagerness to learn. As always, there were some who swayed hesitantly in the background or others who stood still, not participating at all. Those were often the ones who needed her the most.

"Miss Tyne, can you do this move?"

Haley smiled and joined in, pretending to fumble the step and allowing the girl to teach her. The confidence boost and proud smile that came with the lesson always brought a warmth to her chest.

"Okay, class, listen up. One last spectacular move and we'll switch to cool-downs before we call it a day. You've all done amazing for your first class."

Haley nodded to her assistant, Rowan, an energetic sixteen-year-old who was volunteering here for the summer. Rowan's brother attended the camp and Rowan was hoping to go to dance college in a couple of years, so they were a great fit for the assistant role. Rowan moved to grab Haley's phone and bring up the cool-down playlist as a piercing cry greeted Haley's ears. Her head swivelled around until it landed on a young girl, lying on the floor, and surrounded by both panicked and curious peers.

"Make space, please, move back," Haley said as she manoeuvred through the throng to get to the girl. She wasn't quite there with everyone's names yet. Only the kids who demanded attention usually stuck quickly, and this girl hadn't been one of them.

"She tripped over Billie's leg and fell, and I think her leg is broken 'cause she won't move," one of the kids rambled as Haley crouched down close to the girl. She did not want to deal with a broken limb in her first class of this camp. The girl was curled in a ball with hands over her ears and eyes staring straight ahead.

"Hey there, you okay?" Haley asked softly.

She scanned her eyes over the girl's legs to see if anything looked broken. Apart from a scrape that would need cleaning, nothing appeared out of place.

"Rowan, can you take everyone over there to go through the cool-down, please?" Haley kept her voice soft and even and was grateful when Rowan immediately sprang into action, wrangling the gawking kids away to the other side of the large gym.

"There's a room over through that door on the right that has a first aid kit, and it's much quieter. Do you think you could walk over there?"

The girl didn't react for a moment as she sat with her hands still clamped over her ears, but Haley gave her time to process what she had said. A moment later she gave a small nod and Haley moved to stand.

"Do you need help getting up?"

The sharp shake of the girl's head let Haley know that she most likely didn't want to be touched, which Haley suspected. Her only concern was if there was any sprain to her leg, walking unaided could cause an issue. Her fears were short lived, though, as the girl walked toward the door without more than a wince and Haley followed her inside.

"You can sit on that chair, and I'll grab the first aid supplies. That scrape on your leg needs a clean, but that's all I can see. Is there pain anywhere else?"

The girl shook her head, to Haley's relief. A scrape and

overstimulation she could deal with. Haley had set this room up before the camp started specifically for incidents like this. It had low lighting and a range of chairs and bean bags as well as a box of sensory toys and fidgets. There was a basic first aid kit in the cupboard. Anyone that required more would be sent to their on-staff nurse at the makeshift clinic they had in the main building.

"Is there anything I can get for you?"

If Haley hadn't been looking at the girl's mouth move, she wouldn't have noticed her reply at all. The barely whispered word got lost in the space between them.

"I'm sorry, I can't hear you. Do you want to try again, or I have a pen and paper if you want to write?"

"Kay."

The word was clearer now, but it still didn't bring Haley any closer to understanding its meaning. The door opened then, and Rowan popped their head in, glancing between them.

"The kiddos are all gone to their next class now, we've got about an hour before the next group come in. Do you need anything here?"

Haley glanced back at the girl, wishing she had remembered to implement name tags for the first class, and saw her gaze move over and up to Rowan's.

"Kay," she said again, this time directing the word Rowan's way.

"I'll get her, I think she's close by," Rowan replied with a smile. Haley's face must have portrayed her confusion as Rowan added, "Her sister Cadhla works here, I think she's in the lunchroom prepping. I'll go ask her to pop over."

Haley was even more grateful for Rowan in that moment and mouthed her thanks as she turned back to the task at hand. She pulled an antiseptic wipe packet from the small green box along with a band aid and some cream. She held up the antiseptic wipe packet and grimaced.

"Okay, not gonna lie, this one is going to sting like a…thing that stings. Do you want to do it yourself, or will I?"

A hint of a smile graced the girl's face, and she took the packet from Haley to rip it open. She quickly swiped it across the cut on her knee to clean the now dried blood away and didn't even flinch.

"Well, clearly you're braver than me. I hate those things. Now, do you want to let it air out or hide it with a plaster?"

The girl's eyes flicked up to her as she took the Band-Aid from the table.

"Minor cuts should be covered so that they can heal properly and to prevent the new surface cells that are being created from drying out." The girl's voice was strong now, and she had more colour returning to her face.

"Good to know," Haley replied as a voice piped up from behind her.

"You already causing havoc and correcting people, May?"

Rowan had left the door ajar on her way out, so Haley hadn't heard the newcomer, presumably the girl's sister, enter. Haley turned with a big smile that swiftly faded as her mouth fell open in surprise.

"Cal."

The woman who had played a starring role in so many of her dreams for the past almost two years stood before her now, without a hint of recognition on her face.

"Kay."

The simple word was a reminder to Haley of their current circumstances, and she snapped back into action, stepping out of the way to allow Cal to move toward her sister.

"You okay, Maeve? What happened?"

Haley busied herself in the corner tidying up the supplies she'd taken out of the cupboard to get the first aid kit.

"I fell. Which was fine, it's only a scrape, but everyone surrounded me, and they were all talking so loudly, and I couldn't move. I froze."

Maeve confirmed Haley's suspicions as to the real cause of the panic earlier, and Haley glanced over at Cal's face, which was full of concern.

Or is it Kay? Was the name she gave that night fake?

"That sucks. Do you want to go back to the cabin and lie down for a while?"

Maeve shook her head emphatically as Haley glanced between them.

"No, I'm good. I want to go. I just panicked but I got a handle on it. Miss Tyne helped me."

Cal glanced Haley's way then and back to Maeve.

"You sure, May? I'm sure someone can cover for me for a while, and we can watch a—"

"I said I'm good. I don't need to be babied, okay? I'm going to my next class now, and you have work to get back to."

Haley's eyebrows rose at the force behind Maeve's words as she hopped up from the chair and made her way toward the door.

"Hey, you called me here, so drop the attitude. I'm only trying to help."

Maeve stood with her hand on the door and Haley's eyes bounced between them, any pretence of keeping herself busy gone.

"I know I called you. I was scared. But I'm telling you I'm okay now. Just trust me, please."

Haley watched the mix of emotions that flitted across Cal's face. There was obviously more going on beneath the surface level of this conversation, and Haley's curiosity was piqued.

"Okay, just check in with me after your next class, and if it gets too much, come find me. Promise?"

Maeve smiled before replying, "I promise."

She made her way out the door that swung shut behind her and left Cal standing there staring after it.

"She'll be okay," Haley found herself saying without even considering it.

Cal nodded softly before she replied.

"Yeah, I just worry about her. She has so much to deal with, and she's just a kid."

Haley stared at her a moment as Cal's eyes stayed trained upon the door. Clearly, despite Haley uttering the name, Cal had no idea who she was. For all Haley knew, she didn't even remember the fake name she had given Haley at Willow's, and she had been too focused on her sister to hear Haley say it. That was a good thing, right? Haley had a chance to pretend like they were nothing more than two strangers meeting today, which would make bumping into each other around camp for the next few weeks infinitely less awkward.

"She seems like a capable kid to me. She calmed herself quickly, far quicker than I knew how to do at that age. I know it's not my place to say and I don't know all the ins and outs, but…don't make her regret calling you for help when she needs to."

Cal's eyes landed on Haley's then, and the piercing slate grey depths sent a jolt through her. Haley hoped her face gave nothing away as the dormant butterflies in her stomach came to life.

"You don't know her," Cal said.

"I don't. But she does," Haley said as she gestured toward the door Maeve had exited through. She turned to tidy up the first aid kit and tried to ignore the heat of Cal's stare. Silence enveloped the room as Haley closed the cupboard and turned. She was startled by Cal still standing there staring. They stood for a moment, just looking at each other, and Haley wondered if the sound of her heart thumping was as loud to Cal as it was to her.

"I should get ready for my next class," Haley said. As she moved toward the door, Cal did the same, and they wound up facing each other as they both reached toward the handle. The low lighting of the space suddenly became more apparent, and if Haley didn't know any better, she would've sworn the room had shrunk from only moments ago. Time stood still as the intensity she had remembered so well buzzed between them, before Cal stepped back and gestured toward the door.

"After you," Cal said.

Her silky tone gave no indication that she was feeling any of the overwhelming feelings that coursed through Haley's body.

Get a grip, Tyne.

Haley scolded herself as she walked through the door and blinked as she stepped into the much brighter gym. She needed to push those feelings far, far down and forget they ever existed, much the way Cal clearly had. This camp was important, and the last thing she needed was to ruin it by pining over someone who had already unknowingly taken up too much of her time.

"Hey, I didn't say thanks, by the way. For helping Maeve."

Cal spoke as she walked backward toward the gym entrance.

"She seems like a great kid," Haley replied.

Cal smiled then, a genuine smile that softened her features and made Haley's traitorous heart squeeze.

"She really is. Thanks, Miss Tyne. Or should I say Trouble?"

Cal winked with her parting word and walked out the door as Haley stood there with her mouth wide open.

Well, shit.

CHAPTER EIGHT

"Earth to Cal, it's your sister calling."
Maeve waved her hand in front of Cal's face as Cal snapped out of the daze she had found herself in most of the day.

"What's up with you today? You're being weirder than usual, which is an accomplishment."

Maeve grinned widely at her own joke as Cal shook her head.

"You're hilarious," Cal said as she picked up her fork and stabbed at her now cold food.

"Yes I am, thank you for noticing. But really, you've been off since earlier. Are you mad that I wouldn't go lie down? I'm fine, and I haven't had another issue since dance class."

Cal looked at Maeve then and saw her clearly for probably the first time all day. She looked happier than she had in a long time.

"I'm not mad at you, May. Did you have a good day?"

Cal sat back as Maeve excitedly recounted her day, successfully distracted from probing further into Cal's demeanour. Not that Maeve had the background to put two and two together as to what had thrown Cal all afternoon. No, the only person besides Cal with that information was sitting two tables ahead and to the right of them, which so happened to be the direction Cal's eyes kept gazing off to.

Trouble.

The only moniker she could identify the woman with before today. The nickname had played a significant role in the ongoing fantasies Cal had had since their one and only encounter. And calling her *Miss Tyne* evoked just as many fantasies, if not more.

"You're gone again. What's so interesting over there?"

Cal's cheeks heated as Maeve turned her head in the direction that Cal's eyes had wandered to again and she scrambled to think of a believable reply. "Nothing I was just in my head, I wasn't looking at anything in particular."

Maeve looked back at her and shrugged, unbothered by the evasiveness.

"Whatever. I'm done anyway, and I presume you're not gonna eat that very cold stew now. Can we go get ready for the quiz?"

Maeve got up without waiting for a reply and started to clear off her plate as Cal did the same. She had completely forgotten about tonight's table quiz, which was part of the evening entertainment that the camp put on most weekend nights. Cal groaned internally at the realization that she couldn't curl up in bed and pretend to watch something while sorting through her thoughts.

"Hey, Miss Tyne. Thanks again for earlier."

Cal's head shot up and she saw that Maeve had stopped at the table that had taken so much of Cal's attention that evening.

"You're welcome, Maeve, I'm glad you're feeling better. And you can call me Haley."

That last part was said with a slight glance in Cal's direction. Cal bit back the words that almost left her lips. Something along the lines of Trouble suiting her better, but it was not the time or the place. It hadn't been earlier that day either, but the words had been out before Cal could stop them.

"This is my sister, by the way," Maeve said as she pointed to Cal before continuing. "Oh wait, I forgot you met already."

Cal almost laughed at the widening of Haley's eyes and the panicked look thrown her way.

"But I forgot to introduce you then so I should do it now. Her name is Cadhla, but nobody calls her that. It's spelled in the Irish way C-A-D-H-L-A and not the K-A-Y-L-A way. Most people call her Cal and sometimes I call her Kay. Like earlier."

Haley visibly relaxed as she realized Maeve was referring to their earlier meeting that day and not the one that clearly came to mind for them both. Cal smiled at Maeve's familiar rambling of information and was comforted by the fact that Haley didn't seem in the least bothered by it.

"Nice to officially meet you, Cal," Haley said and held out her hand in a gesture that caught Cal off guard. Cal slipped her hand into Haley's smaller one, and her body had an immediate response to the contact.

"You too, Haley."

Cal drew the name out, enjoying the look on Haley's face as it left her lips. As Haley's grip on her hand loosened, Cal had to stop herself from trying to hold on just a little longer. What kind of magic did this person have over her?

"Since Haley has forgotten all of her manners, I'll introduce myself. I'm Branna."

Cal had been so consumed with Haley that she hadn't paid any attention to the other occupant of the table. Not that it was a problem anyway because when she did finally glance at the young girl, Branna's eyes and smile were directed solely at Maeve.

"You're in my group for STEM, right?" Maeve asked softly.

Well, that's interesting.

There was a shyness there that Cal hadn't seen before. Maeve had a good, albeit small, group of friends at home that she was comfortable with, but Cal hadn't seen her hesitant like this around a peer before. And if she wasn't mistaken, her sister was sporting a blush.

"Yep. I remember you knew a lot of stuff already and it's only our first day. You're smart."

That was definitely a blush. Cal glanced at Haley, who glanced back at her with a look of amusement.

"Oh hey, are you coming to the quiz later?" Branna asked.

"I, we, yeah. I mean yes."

Cal almost laughed out loud at Maeve's mumbled reply. She hadn't heard her sister mumble anything in her life. Cal was used to Maeve going silent in times of stress or overload, but apart from that Maeve was always confident and direct with her words.

"Cool. We should be on a team, if you don't have one already, I mean. I already convinced Haley to pair with me, so we need two more. My friends don't get here for another week, so Hales is stuck with me for now."

"That's her way of saying she's only using my company until something better comes along." Haley laughed as she threw an affectionate look Branna's way.

"Can we? Please?" Maeve whispered up at Cal with a pleading look on her face. Cal's thoughts raced and she didn't have time to consider all angles right now. Spending the evening in a group with someone she already had a complicated, if brief, history with was probably not the best idea. But there was no way she could be the one to wipe that hopeful look off Maeve's face.

"If Haley is good with it, then I am."

All eyes moved Haley's way then, and a mix of emotions flitted across her face. Cal couldn't think of a logical reason for Haley to give not to be okay with it, and she had a feeling Haley was coming to the same conclusion.

"Yeah, sure."

The agreement caused a wide smile to cross Maeve's face. To Cal's surprise, the moment Maeve became aware of it she tried to replace it with a more neutral look. Hiding her feelings was something Maeve had never been very good at, and Cal was glad that wasn't changing anytime soon. The fact that Branna's smile was almost as wide seemed to give Maeve some comfort.

They made plans to meet in the hall before the quiz and then Cal and Maeve headed back to the staff dormitories. The camp was on the grounds of an old boarding school, and the room she would call home for the rest of the summer housed two twin beds, a dresser and an ensuite toilet. It was small, but still more than Cal had expected. Maeve had her own assigned bed in the shared dorms on the other side of the building but had slept here with Cal since their first night. Maeve knew she was more than welcome to stay any or all nights she might need. As much as Cal wanted Maeve to get the full camp experience, she also knew that selfishly she would sleep a lot better being able to keep an eye on Maeve.

"How did you know you were a lesbian?"

The question caught Cal off guard as they got to the room and Maeve hopped onto the bed she had claimed the night they arrived. The hint of shyness and reddened cheeks that had appeared back in the dinner hall were now gone and Maeve stared at her expectantly.

"Um, I guess I just noticed that I had feelings for girls the way that most of my friends used to talk about feeling for boys."

Maeve pondered her response and Cal set about pulling out clothes to change into for the quiz. She knew the conversation wouldn't end there. It didn't take a detective to figure out where the line of questioning came from, but Cal wanted to give Maeve space to work through her thoughts and feelings without adding any pressure to it.

"Did you ever like boys that way and then it stopped?"

Cal set down the clothes and hopped up on her bed before turning to face Maeve. She jumped between not wanting to scare Maeve off talking to her about these things by making it too serious, but also wanting Maeve to know she had her full attention. Not for the first time, Cal wished there was some sort of manual or guidebook on how to approach heavy topics with kids. Maeve looked up to her, and as much as Cal loved being an important figure for her sister, she also worried about getting it wrong and the impact her words or opinions could have on Maeve's impressionable, still-forming brain.

"No, not really. I had lots of friends that were boys and I enjoyed hanging out with them, and for a while I thought maybe that's all anyone meant when they said they had a crush. And then…"

Cal trailed off as memories of her first crush popped back into her brain. She hadn't thought about her in years.

"And then? You can't leave it at that," Maeve said as she scooched closer to the edge of the bed.

"And then I met Leah. She was the new girl in my class, and everyone was enraptured by her. For a while, I figured that was what was causing those pesky butterflies in my stomach, just curiosity about someone new. But every time she was around, my words seemed to fail me, and my palms would get sweaty, and although

I had nothing to compare it to, I realized that's what a crush really felt like."

Cal smiled as the tinge of pink made its way back onto Maeve's cheeks.

"What age were you?" Maeve asked as her legs bounced unconsciously.

"About your age."

Maeve was silent for a moment before she nodded and got up. That was the end of the conversation for now and Cal sighed in relief.

"I'm going to get dressed now and then we better go. It takes six minutes to get to the hall and the planned meeting time is in twenty minutes."

Cal snorted as she gathered up the clothes from where she had dropped them.

"Yes, yes. Who needs a watch when I've got you around to keep me on time," Cal said.

"Well, somebody's got to," Maeve retorted.

It took everything in Cal not to ask Maeve outright about how she was feeling and if this was about Branna, but she knew her sister. Maeve would speak about it when she was ready to speak about it, and questioning her before she was ready would only make her retreat. The conversation had gone as well as it could have, and Cal needed to trust herself, and Maeve for that matter. Plus, at least the distraction of the talk had left no room for Cal to dwell on the fact that she was about to go spend hours next to the woman who had unknowingly been an integral part of one of the most significant nights of her life. Haley, who now had a name to add to the face that had floated its way into her dreams on more than one occasion.

CHAPTER NINE

Haley watched the double doors to the hall open and close to yet another teenager eagerly scanning the room for their group. They had about five minutes before the time they had agreed to meet Cal and Maeve, but Haley was in waiting mode so she couldn't focus on anything else. Branna was oblivious while engrossed in her phone and was no help as a distraction.

It had been a packed day of classes and getting to know all the groups had left little time for Haley to dwell on the curveball that came in the shape of her tall, dark, and gorgeous one-night fling. The last person in the world Haley had expected to run into here of all places. She had gone almost two years without ever bumping into Cal again, and even though Haley had avoided Willow's, the city they both lived in wasn't big. So to travel away from there and bump into Cal here hadn't even been on a list of concerns for her camp experience.

Is it a concern?

It was a question Haley had been thinking of in the little bits of time she stole for herself today. In reality, they were two people who shared a flirty evening together. Cal had no idea that she was a catalyst for Haley's coming out to her mother and accepting herself, and that she played an integral role in Haley's story. If Haley kept that information to herself, then there was no reason they couldn't get through this camp just fine. Sure, Haley had been disappointed not to hear anything from Cal after their night, but Cal didn't owe her anything.

"Oh, hey, they're here," Branna piped up as she set her phone on the table.

The action made Haley smile. Maybe being engrossed in her phone had been a ruse after all to hide the fact that Branna had been in waiting mode as much as Haley had been. It was an adorable development as Branna's leg bounced anxiously while Maeve and Cal neared their table.

"Sorry we're late, blame her," Maeve said with a glare at Cal.

"We're not late. We're exactly on time," Cal replied before shaking her head in exasperation.

"A minute ago would've been exactly on time," Maeve huffed right at the same time as Branna piped up and said, "You're technically one minute late."

Haley laughed and Cal slid into the empty seat beside her since Maeve had occupied the one nearest Branna.

"Double trouble. They're ganging up on me," Cal stage-whispered to Haley.

"I mean, technically they're both right," Haley stage-whispered back, and Maeve smiled smugly.

"Oh, no, not you too," Cal replied with a groan.

"Sorry, facts are facts," Haley said with a shrug.

"Triple trouble it is, then," Cal mumbled.

Haley raised her eyebrows at the statement as Cal heard her own words and grinned. The camp leaders who were on entertainment duty for the evening passed by to hand out answer sheets and pens to each team. Cal got the designated role of writer of answers since she had the most legible handwriting, and then the quiz was underway.

"How in the world did you know the answer to that?" Cal asked Haley in amazement as she correctly answered one of the more obscure questions of the night.

"I have ADHD. I can't remember what I'm on the way to do most days, but I have a lot of space in my brain filled with random facts," Haley replied.

"I can concur. My ADHD brain also likes to remember random facts but neglects to remember that my friends exist sometimes. It's a trip," Branna said as Cal laughed.

Between Haley's random facts, Maeve's abundance of general knowledge, Cal's scarily accurate guesses, and Branna's input with pop culture, they were the highest scoring team at the end of the quiz. They cheered and gladly accepted their prize of chocolate and little plastic trophies.

"This is going to take pride of place on my bedside locker," Haley said as she held up the trophy triumphantly.

"I'm going to head back to the dorms now and do the same with mine. Make sure everyone remembers what a kick-ass quiz expert they are bunking with," Branna said as she pushed back her chair.

"What dorm are you in? Want to walk back with me?" Branna asked Maeve and Cal's head shot up.

"I'm in the Green dorm, but I stayed in Cal's so far, so I'm not sure where it is yet. Cal dropped my bag over while I was in orientation," Maeve replied.

"It's right next to mine, I can show you," Branna said with a smile.

Haley's interest was piqued at the growing concern on Cal's face at the conversation.

"You left some of your stuff in my room. We can go back and get it and I can walk you to the dorms then if you want to go," Cal said.

"It's nothing important, I can grab it in the morning," Maeve replied as she hopped up from her chair. Cal looked like she wanted to say more but stayed quiet as they both waved and headed toward the door.

"Branna is a good kid, I promise. Maeve is safe with her."

Haley offered the words to Cal knowing it wouldn't ease all of her concerns, but hopefully it would provide some comfort.

"She seems great. That's not what I'm worried about. It's just… Maeve hasn't stayed anywhere without me since I moved back," Cal spoke the words softly, still staring toward the door that they had left through as if debating whether to follow.

"She's lucky to have such a supportive big sister. But there are leaders staying in each dorm, and they'll know how to reach you if she needs you. It'll be in the care plans that were submitted for each camper."

Cal nodded a couple of times before focusing on Haley. It was only then that Haley realized they were alone now. Well, alone at the table, since the hall was still busy with people chatting and making their way out.

"Do you want to take a walk?"

Haley startled herself with the words. Why had she suggested that? The hall was a safe, neutral zone surrounded by people which is what Haley should want right now with Cal.

"Yeah, I'd like that. If I go right back to my room, I'll just be trying to convince myself not to take Maeve's stuff over there as an excuse to check on her."

Cal laughed as they got up and headed outside. The sky was darkening, but being summer it was still bright enough to see clearly. They walked in silence for a while toward the fenced lake behind the gym hall, which had a footpath circled around it.

"So, of all the camps in all of Ireland…how'd you end up here?" Cal asked, breaking the silence between them.

"Well, it was actually Branna that got me the gig. She's been coming to my mom's dance school since she was little, and I've been teaching her since I started working there. She came here last year and adored it. They were looking for a dance coordinator for this year, so Branna floated my name to the organizer and that was that. Like I mentioned before, I have ADHD. So it seemed like a good fit for me. Being able to teach kids who had similar struggles as I did growing up felt right. Dance was always an escape for me, and I want to help other kids find that too."

Haley looked over at Cal after a minute passed without reply only to find Cal staring back at her.

"What?" Haley asked as her cheeks heated under the intense look.

"That's a good answer. You're going to make a real difference to the kids here," Cal whispered as her eyes searched Haley's before looking forward again. Haley flushed under the sincerity of the words.

"Thank you. I hope so. What about you, what brings you here other than your overprotectiveness?" Haley joked.

"I mean, that's pretty much the reason. Well, that and my working here means Maeve gets to attend. As awesome as this place is, it's not exactly cheap. So part of the options they offer for people who want it is working here in exchange for a free place along with the basic wages. It's not much, but with board and food covered for us for the duration, it'll cover what I'm losing from my job back home. Luckily, there's plenty of college kids looking for summer bar work, so it was easy to get cover to take the month off."

It was Haley's turn to stare in admiration as Cal shrugged.

"That's really great of you. I don't know many siblings who would offer to work in a camp full of hormonal teenagers for over a month just to help their sister get a place here."

Cal furrowed her brow as if uncomfortable with what Haley had said.

"It's not that big a deal. Maeve deserves to get the same experience as anyone else would," Cal said.

"She does. But just because she deserves it doesn't mean it isn't great of you to actually make sure she gets it. She's lucky to have you looking out for her," Haley pressed, as Cal turned to look out toward the lake.

"Well, I haven't always done a great job at that, so I have a lot to make up for."

Haley could hear the heaviness in Cal's words and had to stop herself from reaching out to take Cal's hand. It was bizarre walking next to someone who was still so much of a stranger, but to whom Haley felt such a connection.

"Do you want to sit for a minute?" Cal asked, pointing toward a bench up ahead facing the lake.

Haley nodded her agreement, and they walked toward the wooden bench covered in carved initials from years of previous occupants.

"It's weird, right, that we both ended up here?" Haley said. She had always been the one to point out elephants in rooms and figured it was about time they addressed this one.

"You mean because we haven't seen each other since the night you seduced me against the wall of my workplace?"

Haley's mouth fell open at Cal's reply before they both burst into laughter.

"Well, that's one way to put it."

Haley leaned back against the bench, properly relaxing for the first time since Cal had walked into her dance class that day.

"What's the other way?" Cal teased as she turned to face Haley.

"I mean, we could call it the night you ghosted me," Haley retorted. She added a smile and hoped it kept her words as light as she intended but Cal's face sobered and Haley regretted saying anything at all.

"I'm kidding. You made your stance clear that night, and I promised no expectations. I'm just glad to find out I won't be contacted by a cold case unit investigating your disappearance in ten years' time."

Cal smiled but it didn't reach her eyes. Eyes that were now a darker grey than usual, filled with something Haley couldn't quite decipher, but it wasn't good.

"Hey, Cal, I didn't mean to dampen the mood or anything. It's cool."

Haley reached out then to cover Cal's hand with hers, and Cal's eyes followed the action.

"I did intend to message you. Things came up and I just… anyway, I wasn't trying to ghost you."

Cal's voice was soft, and it made Haley want to pull her close and hold her until whatever had caused this emotion disappeared. Which would be a terrible idea given the way her body reacted to their hands touching.

"It's okay. It's in the past. How about we call this a fresh start, and we can forget about it?"

Cal's gaze moved up to meet Haley's again and she gulped at the intensity of the moment.

"You want to forget about it?" Cal said, her eyes never wavering from Haley's. Memories flashed through Haley's mind of their bodies pressed together as they danced, and as they kissed. Heat spread through Haley at the images still so vivid in her head.

"Well, maybe not all of it," Haley whispered as she bit her lip to stop a whimper from escaping as Cal's thumb brushed back and forth across her hand.

"You really are trouble, you know that?" Cal said as if the words slipped out of their own accord. She pulled her hand back slowly with a shake of her head, and Haley willed her not to put the distance between them that she knew was coming.

"I should head back. I need to be up early for breakfast duty. Hungry kids and all," Cal said as she stood. Haley followed suit and they began walking back toward the staff dorms in silence. It was a comfortable kind of silence despite it being loaded with the chemistry they clearly shared.

"This is me," Haley said as she pointed toward the ground floor corridor. They stopped walking and Cal turned to face her.

"I'm up on floor two. How'd you snag a ground floor room?" Cal asked with a mock frown.

"I'm charming," Haley said with a grin.

"Don't I know it," Cal mumbled, which made Haley's grin widen. They stood staring at each other for a moment. Haley needed to get out of there before she said something she would, or maybe wouldn't, regret.

"You going to be safe making it up two floors alone?" Haley asked as she began to walk backward toward her door.

"You're very concerned with my safety. Did they put you down here as the first line of defence?" Cal replied as she opened the door to the hall that housed the stairs and elevator to the upper floors.

"Yep. I'm stronger than I look, remember," Haley said before turning to walk to the door. She knew without even looking that Cal's eyes were following her the whole way.

CHAPTER TEN

W hy don't you have a girlfriend?"
Cal opened one eye and peeked across the room to where Maeve had just let herself in.

Note to self: Lock bedroom door at night.

"Seriously May, it's like"—Cal paused to glance at her bedside clock—"seven in the morning. Maybe start with a hello, or even better, a knock on the door."

Maeve flopped down on the bed opposite Cal and switched on the lamp beside it.

"Why would I knock when the door is open and I can just come in?"

Cal groaned and rubbed at her sleepy eyes knowing she wouldn't get the chance to fall back into the wonderful dream she was having. A dream that included a certain person who had been on Cal's mind all week. Cal's schedule had been so busy at the camp that she had barely gotten more than a fleeting glance of Haley since they parted ways at the weekend.

"Because it's polite to knock. What if I wasn't alone?" Cal mumbled.

"That brings us back to my original question. Why don't you have a girlfriend?"

"I like being single," Cal replied.

Maeve scrutinized her for a moment as Cal swung her legs out of the bed and sat up.

"I don't think that's the truth. But I don't know why you'd lie. Women like you, right? And you like them. I remember you had a girlfriend before, but that was a long time ago."

Maeve was fidgeting, and Cal took a moment to consider her reply.

"I'm not trying to lie, but sometimes the truth is too complex to explain easily," Cal said.

"The truth is always easier to understand than trying to figure out if someone is lying or why," Maeve replied.

It was far too early in the morning for these kinds of conversations, but they didn't come from nowhere. She didn't want Maeve to be afraid to speak to her about things in whatever way she needed to get it out.

"As always, you're right, little May. It's early in the morning and I just woke up, so my brain needs time to adjust to being awake. We can have a longer chat about this later if you want. Is everything okay?"

Maeve was quiet for a moment, and it hit Cal suddenly how grown up she had gotten. Even the short time they'd been at camp had affected her sister in a way Cal couldn't quite put her finger on.

"I think so. I guess I wondered how people decide they should have a girlfriend or not. If they are ready. And then that made me think about you and why you don't have one, so I came and asked because that's the best way to find out information."

Cal smiled as she got up and grabbed her wash bag to start getting ready.

"It is, and not enough people realize that. You're a smart cookie, you know that?"

"Mom says I get that from you. She says I get a lot from you."

Cal left the door ajar to the bathroom as she washed up to continue the conversation.

"I think I get as much from you as you do from me, little May. But you're still young, you have plenty of time to worry about dating. You don't need to figure it out right now, you know?"

Cal was met with silence for long enough to make her worry she had said the wrong thing. After brushing her teeth, Cal peeked her head out the bathroom door to make sure Maeve was still in the room.

"You okay?" Cal asked as Maeve glanced up at her.

"I'm just thinking. I know I'm young, but what if I *want* to figure it out?"

Cal emerged from the bathroom and walked over to her sister. She took a seat beside her on the bed and held a hand out to let Maeve decide if she wanted to hold it or not. Maeve's smaller hand slid into hers and Cal squeezed lightly.

"Then we will figure it out. I'm not an expert on the best way to talk to your kid sister about relationships. In fact, I'm not much of an expert on relationships in general. But I promise you can ask whatever questions you want later, and I'll do my best to answer them honestly. But sometimes the honest answer might be that I don't have an answer, so we may be figuring some of it out together, okay?"

Maeve sat with that for a minute before nodding as she checked her watch.

"I need to get going. I have dance first thing, so I only have time for cereal for breakfast."

Cal laughed and grabbed her bag as they left to walk to the cafeteria.

"Cal?"

Cal glanced over at Maeve as they walked and waited for her to continue.

"For someone who isn't an expert, you're still pretty good at it. Talking to me, I mean."

Cal's heart filled with warmth as Maeve's words sank in. Maeve rarely said anything she didn't mean, so the sincerity always made any compliment that much more meaningful to Cal.

They finished up a quick breakfast and Maeve gathered her stuff for dance class.

"I'll walk you over," Cal said as she piled their bowls and cups onto the tray.

"But aren't you working in the cafeteria this morning?" Maeve asked as they headed toward the doors.

"Yeah, but I don't start till after the breakfast rush. I'm on clean-up duty and lunch prep, so I have time."

Cal had plenty she could be doing to make her morning easier, but accompanying Maeve meant potentially seeing Haley. An ulterior motive she would not mention to her sister, especially with their most recent conversations.

"It's interesting how you only seem to wanna accompany me anywhere when it involves Miss Tyne."

Busted.

Apparently, Cal hadn't been as subtle about her intentions as she had hoped.

Cal hummed in response, not wanting to deny anything but unwilling to confirm it either.

"She asks about you too. I think sometimes adults think I won't pick up on stuff because I'm a kid, or maybe because I'm autistic. Which is silly because I excel at pattern recognition. Not that I'd need to with the way you guys so obviously flirt. Branna notices too."

Heat crept up Cal's face as they neared the gym, and Maeve looked over at her.

"Your cheeks are red now. Is it because I noticed the flirting or because you're thinking about Miss Tyne?"

Maeve grinned widely as Cal glared at her and willed her cheeks to cool.

"You get that sass from me too, you know. So be careful or I might have to return the favour."

Cal glanced ahead where Branna waved at them and stopped, presumably waiting for Maeve to catch up. Maeve replicated Cal's glare so accurately Cal couldn't help but laugh.

"I'll play nice if you will, kiddo."

"Deal," Maeve muttered as they fell into step with Branna and Cal faded into the background.

As they got to the gym, the girls waved goodbye to Cal and ran inside to join the small group already forming around Rowan. Cal glanced around the hall and was disappointed not to see Haley anywhere. Haley didn't run every dance class of the camp, but Cal had gotten her hopes up.

"Looking for someone?"

Cal swivelled around and couldn't stop the smile that spread quickly at the sight of Haley walking toward her. Haley's hair was slicked back in a high ponytail and her eyes twinkled as she stopped in front of Cal.

"Sort of," Cal said as she failed to think of a better cover-up.

"Sort of?" Haley echoed.

"Well, I just walked over with Maeve," Cal mumbled as her eyes dipped to the glossy lips she had been thinking about kissing almost nonstop since the weekend.

"Right. And you just wanted to hang around outside and make sure you sealed your overprotective-sister title, huh?" Haley teased.

"Nope. I was hoping to see you. And here you are. But don't you have a class to go teach?" Cal kept her voice light and casual as the truth spilled out.

"Rowan starts the warm-ups for me, so I have a little time. Let's get back to the hoping to see me part," Haley said.

"Well, our schedules seem to have been opposite break wise, so we haven't seen each other since the weekend. I know how much you worry about my safety, so I figured I'd be a Good Samaritan and make sure you knew I was alive. Although you already knew that because you asked Maeve, right?"

Haley studied Cal for a moment before shrugging softly.

"I might have. But at least I didn't go in the opposite direction of where I should be this morning just on the off chance of laying eyes on you and then claim chivalry when caught in the act."

Haley's teasing tone sent shivers through Cal that left her struggling to conjure the right words to deflect with humour.

"How'd you know where I'm scheduled to be this morning?" Cal asked.

Deflection with a question would have to do.

"I checked the schedule. See, honesty isn't so hard. You can just say you wanted to see me, and it won't kill you, I promise."

"I should get going. I have kids to clean up after."

Cal didn't move, and Haley studied her quietly. Cal wasn't sure if it was disappointment on her face or if Cal was projecting. Either way, Cal felt more seen by Haley than she had by anyone in a long time.

"Maybe I'll see you later," Haley said as she stepped to the side and put space between them.

"I hope so," Cal said. The softening of Haley's features confirmed it had been loud enough for her to catch. As Cal walked away and willed herself not to look back, she hoped it was enough.

Chapter Eleven

Haley spent the better part of the week trying to pull herself out of daydreams involving full lips that tasted as good as they looked. Which made the task of focusing on the words coming from those same lips harder than it should've been.

"Are you listening to anything I'm saying?" Cal asked with a head tilt that indicated she knew exactly what had Haley so distracted.

"Of course I'm listening. You said you're afraid to do tonight's quiz without me on your team in case you lose, and everyone knows I'm the secret weapon."

Haley was thankful for the part of her brain that took in information and relayed it back to her while the other part daydreamed about kissing.

"That's not exactly how I phrased it. Maeve is insistent that we have the same team as last week to defend our title, and so I wanted to check if that was okay with you before I agreed."

"Same difference. You want me on your team is the takeaway here," Haley replied with a grin.

She hadn't seen much of Cal over the week with her busy schedule of classes and planning out the end-of-camp show which Haley would be choreographing. Apart from their not-by-chance run-in outside the dance class that is. But when she had fallen into bed every night, Cal had been at the forefront of her mind before exhaustion pulled her under. Whether it was a smart move or not, Haley wanted to be in her presence tonight.

"Is that a yes, or am I going to have to beg?" Cal said with a pout.

Haley's skin prickled at the thoughts that brought on. Cal's expression told Haley that her face said as much.

"As tempting as that sounds, we have two teens on their way toward us who might ask questions if you start. So I'll put you out of your misery and say yes."

Haley gestured behind Cal to where Branna and Maeve walked toward them through the crowd of kids and staff grabbing tables with their trays of lunch.

"Did you ask?" Maeve said to Cal as they arrived at the table Haley had grabbed for a quick lunch right before Cal had come up and started this conversation.

"She did, and I said yes. We can't break up the winning team," Haley said as a big smile lit up Maeve's face.

Maeve and Branna had been practically glued at the hip since last week's quiz. Haley wondered if that would change when Branna's friends arrived tomorrow, but the way Branna's smile grew when Maeve's smile appeared made Haley think otherwise.

"Cal, I'm going to eat lunch with Branna today over there. So you should sit here with Miss Tyne, and that way you won't be alone," Maeve said matter-of-factly.

"Oh gee, thanks for thinking of me, kiddo. I never would've known what to do with myself otherwise," Cal retorted sarcastically.

"You're welcome," Maeve replied before waving as she walked toward the line for food. It had already doubled in size from when Haley had arrived.

Cal stuck her tongue out at Maeve's retreating form and Haley chuckled as she pushed out the chair across from her.

"Very mature. No wonder she needs to look out for you," Haley said as Cal plopped into the chair. She took what looked suspiciously like a deli bag out of her backpack and placed it on the table in front of them.

"Hold up. You got outside food?" Haley widened her eyes as Cal pulled a chicken and cheese sandwich from the bag. She almost began salivating when it was followed by a cookie that looked like it was fresh from the oven.

"You're not the only one able to woo people with your charms, Haley Tyne," Cal said with a smile.

"Not. Fair. Who do I have to kiss to get a cookie like that?"

The words were out of Haley's mouth before she could think about them, and her face flushed. Cal stopped with the sandwich halfway toward her mouth as her smile widened.

"I don't even care how that sounded, that cookie looks like heaven after a week of cafeteria food. I will say the food standard is better than I expected here, but it's still designed to feed many in a short period of time. No handmade, freshly baked cookies in sight. Until now."

Cal laughed as she chewed her sandwich.

"Don't let Ray hear you dissing his food. You should see what he has to work with back there," Cal said as she pointed toward the kitchen.

"He does a great job, but desserts are clearly not high on the priority list."

Haley continued to drool over the cookie and ignored the unappetizing chocolate pudding on her tray.

"I happen to love chocolate pudding cups. You're underselling it," Cal said after finishing the food in her mouth as she pointed to Haley's tray.

"Then we should trade," Haley said.

"I'm not sure a chocolate pudding cup is a fair trade with this triple chocolate cookie," Cal replied.

"It's *triple* chocolate!" Haley groaned as she shot Cal her best puppy dog eyes. "You're torturing me."

"How about I get your chocolate pudding and we split the cookie?" Cal suggested.

"Deal," Haley replied immediately and stuck out her hand.

Cal laughed as she slid her palm into Haley's, and they shook on it. Haley wouldn't have been surprised if the sparks that flew at the contact were visible to all. They held the handshake a moment longer than normal before Cal cleared her throat and reached for the cookie.

"I hope this lives up to the hype," Cal said as she split the cookie down the middle and passed half along the table to an eagerly waiting Haley.

"Oh my God, this is better than I imagined," Haley said as she devoured every piece.

She licked the last crumb from her lips and looked up to find Cal's eyes fixated on her mouth.

"You gonna eat that?" Haley said as she pulled her bottom lip between her teeth for good measure and pointed toward the second half of the cookie.

"All yours," Cal replied.

She pushed the second half of the cookie over and grabbed the pudding cup from Haley's tray.

"You sure? It's delicious," Haley said, but she barely waited for a reply before popping it into her mouth.

"I'm sure it is. But I couldn't deprive you when you so clearly enjoyed it."

Cal made no move to hide the fact that she was also enjoying watching Haley. The flirtation was fun and light, and Haley tried to remind herself that that's all it was. The ache between her legs would need to get under control if she was going to manage a whole evening of it. Especially when Cal looked like she wanted to devour Haley the way Haley devoured the cookie.

"So you didn't actually tell me, how'd you snag this lunch?" Haley asked.

Cal avoided her gaze as she packed her wrappers back into the paper bag.

"I need to keep some mystery."

"Some? Pretty much everything about you is a mystery, apart from the fact that you're a very caring big sister."

"Not true. You also know where I work," Cal replied.

"True, but that doesn't tell me a lot about who you are."

"What exactly do you want to know?"

Everything.

Haley stopped herself from saying the word and began clearing up her tray.

"Whatever you want to tell me. But I have a class in five minutes, so I need to go now."

Haley emptied her tray into the bin, and they walked toward the door together.

"Maybe we can take another walk later to talk and I can be a little less mysterious. Well, about everything but where I got my lunch. That's a secret you're not getting out of me."

Cal waved goodbye as she headed toward the class she was working in that day. Haley skipped to her dance class and tried not to worry about how excited she was for the quiz to end.

"I can't believe we fell at the last hurdle. Who in the world knew LEGO is the world's largest manufacturer of tires?" Haley said.

They walked toward the lake having just waved Maeve and Branna off to their dorms.

"Well, clearly the team that beat us did. I still say they cheated. One of them had a phone hidden somewhere with Google on it," Cal replied with a huff.

Haley laughed at Cal's furrowed brow.

"So, another thing I now know about you, you're a sore loser."

"Who likes to lose? That's not mysterious. But alas, we'll have to study up and come back swinging next week."

Next week.

Haley stifled a smile as they made their way toward their bench. It was far too soon to name it their bench considering they had only sat here once together. But that's still how Haley thought of it as they approached.

"So, should I be concerned about how much time Branna and Maeve are spending together?" Cal asked after they sat side by side.

"I wouldn't be. They are cute, and it seems like a harmless crush on both sides. I was glued at the hip with my best friend at that age too. Granted, not much has changed there. I'm not sure she's forgiven me yet for disappearing this summer," Haley said with a laugh.

"That must be nice, though. Having someone you've shared so much of your life with," Cal said as she gazed out toward the lake. The reflection of the setting sun illuminated against the almost still water.

"I take it you don't have the same friends as you did when you were her age, then?" Haley asked.

Cal had suggested getting to know each other better, so they might as well start here.

"No. I don't have much of anyone in my life the same as then, apart from my mom. And even she isn't the same person she was when I was thirteen."

The way Cal said it didn't make it sound like it was a bad thing, but Haley's heart still tugged for her.

"I can't imagine that. I've grown up with the majority of the people who are still important in my life now. It was always just me and my mom at home, but her dance studio was my second home and the people there are family. Did you live somewhere else growing up?"

Cal shook her head and then there was silence. Haley didn't want to push and was about to change the subject when Cal finally spoke up.

"We've always lived in the same place, but my home life didn't really breed an environment I wanted to bring people to. I rarely invited friends over, and I wouldn't go to other people's houses. I'd worry about my mom if I was gone. She has struggled with her mental health for a long time, which isn't something people talked about in her family, so it went unmanaged until a couple of years ago."

Haley digested the information as she pictured a young Cal growing up far sooner than she should have. It made sense why she was so protective of Maeve.

"That must have been tough."

The words were an understatement, but it was all Haley could think to offer.

"I'm not sure why I put that all out there. It's not like me," Cal said as her face reddened. She twisted her hands where they lay in her lap.

"It's my charm. It can work like a truth serum. You should be careful around me," Haley replied with a smile. She hoped it eased some of Cal's discomfort.

"I'm glad you told me, though. I get the feeling you've been carrying a lot by yourself for too long."

The look on Cal's face told Haley that she was right. It was as if Cal was surprised to be found out.

"What's your favourite movie?" Cal asked.

"Ah, my favourite kind of conversational segue, random questions with zero relation to the topic at hand," Haley said.

"I find that I forget every movie I've ever seen when someone asks for a favourite. Right now I'll go with *Dirty Dancing* because I'm watching it on repeat in my downtime to prepare for the end of year show."

Cal turned and crossed her legs and Haley mirrored her.

"The end of year show at a kids' summer camp is *Dirty Dancing*?" Cal said with an amused smile.

"Not exactly. It's a combination of a few different musicals so we can incorporate different talents, and we're ending with the *Dirty Dancing* finale dance. Which I'm performing with one of the other dance teachers. Honestly, I've wanted an excuse to learn that dance off for a long time."

Cal laughed and shook her head.

"Better you than me. The idea of doing that in front of the whole camp and their families would terrify me. The idea of watching you do it is far more appealing."

Haley gulped at Cal's flirtatious smile. There was something about being with Cal as the sky grew darker around them that emboldened her.

"Well, I spend most evenings practicing it in the gym, so feel free to drop in. I have no performance anxiety when it comes to dancing."

Cal looked at her for a long moment. Her gaze dropped to Haley's lips before moving back to her eyes. Haley wondered if her own eyes were as lust filled as Cal's. They sat taking each other in as if wondering who would break first, before Cal spoke in a much huskier voice than her normal.

"I think I just might do that."

Chapter Twelve

H ow're my girls doing?"

Cal smiled as her mom walked toward them. Maeve bounced on her heels beside her. They had been watching from Cal's bedroom window that looked out over the car park since after breakfast. Cal's stomach had finally settled as their mom's car came up the driveway.

"Good. It's almost lunch time and we baked stuff for you. Come this way."

Maeve tugged their mom forward without even waiting for a reply as Cal laughed at her eagerness.

"How was the drive?" Cal asked as they walked through the overly crowded courtyard filled with kids and their visitors.

"It was easier than I expected. I'm listening to a new audiobook, so that kept me entertained."

"Miss Tyne! My mom's here today," Maeve yelled excitedly to Haley, who was walking a little ahead of them.

Maeve had taken to Haley over the past couple of weeks, and Cal was grateful that it seemed mutual. Haley waited until they caught up to her and smiled brightly at them all. Her eyes lingered on Cal a moment longer than the rest, and Cal's stomach dipped.

"Hey there. That's great," Haley said to Maeve before turning toward their mom.

"I'm Haley, one of the dance teachers here. It's great to meet you. You have a pretty awesome kid here."

Cal cleared her throat loudly and folded her arms in front of her.

"Just one, eh?" Cal asked.

Haley's eyes twinkled as a small grin appeared on her lips.

"Jury's still out on the other one."

Cal tilted her head to the side and stared at Haley as she feigned hurt.

"And here I thought we were friends."

Haley bit her lip as if stopping words from escaping them. Cal's mom glanced between them and then shot Cal an amused look.

"Good to meet you, Haley. I'm Clara. Are you heading for lunch too? I heard there were baked goods waiting," she said as they began walking toward the cafeteria again.

"Yep, lunch time for me too. I have an easy day today since it's visitor day," Haley replied.

The cafeteria was buzzing with people as they entered. The tables had been decorated with centrepieces made in the art classes, and there were rows of buffet style food along the walls. Maeve led them toward the table laden with cookies, cakes, and biscuits baked by the kids yesterday.

"See, I did these ones," Maeve said as she pointed toward a plate of plain shortbread biscuits.

"My favourite," Clara replied with a smile. They grabbed plates and filled them with food. Cal glanced around looking for a free table before her mom pointed to where Haley had sat down.

"Let's join your *friend*, if she'll have us," Clara said, and she headed in that direction without waiting for a reply.

"Mind if we join you?"

Haley's smile was genuine as she indicated for them to sit. Conversation flowed easily as they caught their mom up on what had been happening at the camp so far.

"Miss Tyne is doing a cool dance for our end of year show. It's from that old movie you like," Maeve said.

"She means *Dirty Dancing*," Cal clarified as they all glared at Maeve.

"Old movie, pfft. It's called a classic, you know."

"Same thing," Maeve said.

"I'm excited to see that. I haven't been to a show in years, probably since Cal stopped dancing. I loved seeing you up on stage," Clara said as she turned to Cal.

Cal averted her eyes and picked at the remaining cookie on her plate. She bit back the immediate retort that came to mind but couldn't stop the words from circling her brain.

Then why did you always forget to show up?

The resentment that still simmered beneath the surface began to rise to the top as Cal recalled exactly why she had stopped dancing. The constant disappointment when nobody showed up to see her perform. The questions from her peers about who would be in the audience. The shame that came from knowing she wasn't as important as her mom's latest love interest.

"You danced?"

Cal registered the question from Haley but was saved from answering when Clara cut in. She seemed oblivious to the memories she had stirred for Cal.

"Oh yeah, she was great. She had such natural rhythm, and she loved it too. She was so dedicated, always dancing around the house."

Cal's discomfort rose as her mom kept talking, and Haley's eyes widened with every word.

"Cal was picked for the lead in those little shows they'd put on and she'd spend ages getting it right. She stopped going as a teenager, but I always wished she'd kept it up. I can't remember the last show she was in, was it *The Wizard of Oz*?"

Haley was glancing from Clara to Cal as if enthralled by this new piece of information.

"*Wizard of Oz* was a few years before. The last one was *Grease*," Cal mumbled.

"Huh. I don't think I remember that one," Clara replied.

"Yeah, you didn't see it," Cal said before she could stop herself.

Realization clicked then and Clara's smile dimmed. Cal got up from the chair and grabbed her tray as she tried to move past the awkwardness of the moment.

"I'm going to dump this and grab a drink. Maeve wanted to show you some of her projects in the science room."

Cal could feel eyes on her as she walked away and deposited the tray in its place. She gripped the edge of the table and took a deep breath. She focused on the air going in through her nose and out through her mouth and willed the memories to go back into their box.

Cal had been so happy to be given the dance captain role of the ensemble in *Grease*, and things had been going well again at home. She had let herself become complacent, which made the crash of disappointment so much worse when she looked out into the audience to be met with another empty seat.

"You okay?"

Cal startled at Haley's voice right behind her. Haley placed a soft hand on the small of Cal's back, and she leaned toward the contact. Her body was seeking any sense of comfort to quiet the noise of her mind.

"I—"

"Time to go, Cal, my projects await," Maeve said as Cal turned. Her mom walked up behind Maeve. She had a smile plastered on her face, but the sadness etched into her features behind it had guilt gnawing at Cal.

They had one day together and then Cal's mom would return to their house alone. Now wasn't the time for rehashing past issues. Cal pushed down her own feelings and smiled at them both.

"Let's get to it then, little May. Thanks for letting us crash your lunch," Cal said to Haley as she ignored the concerned look on Haley's face.

"Anytime. It was great to meet you, I'm sure I'll see you again soon," Haley said to Cal's mom as they waved goodbye.

"She seems really nice," Clara said.

"She is. Cal likes her a lot," Maeve replied with a grin.

Clara laughed as Cal mock scowled, and the sound eased a little of the tension coiled inside Cal.

"Where's Branna today?" Cal asked Maeve as a subtle reminder of their deal. Her sister shot her a wide eyed look that their mom luckily missed.

"Who's Branna?" Clara asked.

"She's Maeve's friend and a student Haley teaches. We've been on a team for the quiz nights here the past couple of weeks," Cal answered to let Maeve know she wasn't planning on torturing her further. Cal wasn't a total asshole and would never tell their mom anything Maeve wasn't comfortable sharing herself.

"I'm trying to figure out if we should be friends or girlfriends. It's still undecided. That's what Cal was hinting at because she's trying to get me back for saying she likes Miss Tyne. Which she does."

Cal had to give credit to their mom, Clara barely missed a step as she took Maeve's words.

"That's a lot of new information. How are you feeling about it?" Clara asked.

"Well, I think Miss Tyne likes Cal too, so I feel like Cal should say so and it would be easier," Maeve replied.

Cal narrowed her eyes as their mom chuckled softly.

"I meant how do you feel about you and Branna," Clara said.

"Oh. Well, I feel a bit confused because I'm not sure what the difference is between liking someone a lot as a friend or liking them as a girlfriend. And Cal hasn't been very helpful yet. I don't think she really understands the difference either. Maybe you can help me after we look at my projects."

Maeve walked ahead to guide them toward the science room and left them both watching her in awe.

"She's not wrong, you know," Clara said softly.

"About me not understanding the difference? You could give me a little more credit than that," Cal scoffed. "I wasn't sure how much to share with her. She's thirteen."

"I meant about telling that girl if you like her. It's pretty obvious to all around, I figured it out in the first two minutes. Plus, you had crushes at thirteen. Even if you were less forthcoming about them with your mother," Clara replied with a laugh.

Cal had had a very different mother at thirteen. The angry teen version of Cal still present somewhere in her mind wanted to let that all out. To remind her mom of all the reasons she couldn't be forthcoming with her about anything growing up. The eggshells she was raised to tiptoe on with a precision no child should ever have to master. But just like the resentment before, Cal pushed down the unresolved anger and smiled as Maeve showed them around the science room.

After an eventful tour of all of Maeve's projects and achievements, they shared a more comfortable meal together. Cal was both relieved and disappointed when Haley didn't appear in the cafeteria for dinner. She introduced her mom to Ray, the camp's main chef, whom Cal had grown close to while being primarily assigned to the cafeteria for her shifts. The hustle and bustle of the cafeteria wasn't far from her usual day shifts at the bar, if you swapped out noisy crowds of women for rowdy teenagers. Ray raved about Cal's skills in the kitchen, and her mom beamed with pride. Cal ignored the twinge that reminded her that her skills came from necessity when the only way to eat a meal that wasn't cereal was to figure it out herself.

Their mom updated them on the latest gossip from her workplace and was sure to add in about how she had spent her evenings at home while they were gone. Alone. It wasn't that Cal didn't want her mom to have a social life outside of them. The fear came from where that social life could lead without Cal there to guide her mom back on track.

Thankfully, Maeve forgot about wanting to talk about relationships with her mom. It was the last topic Cal wanted to broach today, but she made note to talk more with Maeve about it when they were alone. She wanted to do better to support her sister with her new-found curiosity. However, their mom's track record in that department didn't lend itself to light conversation.

"I better hit the road so I can make it home before it gets dark," Clara said as they walked beside the lake after dinner. They walked back toward their mom's car in the car park to see her off.

"See you again in two weeks, and I'll have lots more projects to show you," Maeve said with a wave.

Cal spotted Branna walking back from waving her own visitors off, and the hurried goodbye made more sense. She smiled as Maeve walked to catch up with Branna and turned back to her mom.

"Branna, I'm guessing?" Clara said with a grin.

"Yup. Neither of us are any competition when Branna is around," Cal joked.

"It's good to see her so happy, and comfortable. She really seems to enjoy it here."

Cal nodded her agreement.

"You should take a leaf out of her book. Relax and enjoy yourself."

Cal looked up to see her mom studying her.

"I am enjoying myself," Cal replied. It was the truth. Cal had enjoyed her time here far more than she had expected. Which had a lot more to do with Haley than she'd like to admit.

"Then try the relaxing part. I'm glad you're here for your sister, but she's thriving. And I know you don't quite believe it yet, but I am too. You don't need to worry about us. Try to focus on yourself for once, please. And maybe on that dance teacher who made eyes at you through our whole lunch."

Clara said the last part with a grin and Cal chuckled. She wanted more than anything to believe what her mom was saying. That things were good, that she was okay. But Cal knew all too well how quickly that could change. Being prepared for it made it easier to deal with when it happened.

"I'll try. We'll call during the week, and I'll see you soon."

"You will. I promise. Maybe Haley can bring that sparkle back and help you find your love of dance again. You were always happiest on stage."

Cal's smile was tight as she waved her goodbye. She walked back toward the campus with a heavier heart than she'd had this morning. The reason her mom always saw her happiest on stage was because the happiness came from Cal looking into the audience and seeing her mom there. Her mom had missed all the times she was heartbroken on stage since her absence was the cause. It would take a lot more than a beautiful woman to help heal those wounds.

But Cal was beginning to think Haley could at least help her forget them, if only for a summer.

CHAPTER THIRTEEN

The sweat dripped from Haley as she ran through the second half of the dance. She had spent most of the day since lunch practicing it, and her body ached. The music came to a stop, and only then did Haley's thirst make itself known. Her mind had a habit of blocking out everything else when she hyperfocused, including her body's demands for hydration or toilet breaks.

A soft clap reached her ears as Haley glanced up at the mirror in front of her. She spotted Cal leaning against the wall at the back of the gym.

"How long have you been watching me?" Haley asked as she grabbed her water bottle and took a long gulp. Rather than turn toward Cal, Haley stayed facing her reflection in the mirror.

"Long enough to catch that ridiculously good twist to the choreography in the middle. I'm impressed," Cal said as she pushed off the wall and walked toward Haley.

"Thanks, I'm proud of that part. I've spent most of this afternoon trying to master it."

Haley placed her water bottle down and picked up the towel beside it. She wiped sweat from the easy to reach areas as Cal drew closer.

"You've certainly mastered it. Is that why you missed dinner?"

Haley glanced at the clock on the wall above the mirror and was shocked at the time. She had been in her hyperfocus bubble for longer than she realized.

"Crap, yeah. That wasn't intentional. My body likes to ignore hunger pains when I'm dancing."

Cal was right behind her now. Haley knew that not only from looking in the mirror, but because Cal's breath was right against her neck as she stood as close as they could get without touching. Haley's eyes slid shut momentarily as she willed her body to calm down so she wouldn't spin around and take exactly what she wanted.

Except, why not? Why shouldn't she? They were both grown adults who clearly had chemistry. They had spent the majority of their time together teetering this line with flirting and innuendos. Why were they fighting the pull between them?

Just as Haley talked herself into turning around and facing things head-on, Cal beat her to it. Haley's eyes widened as Cal's hands moved to grip her hips. They locked eyes in the mirror as Cal lowered her mouth and grazed her lips against Haley's bare shoulder. Haley's breath hitched and Cal paused. With their eyes still trained on each other, Haley tilted her head to the side to expose more of her neck. Cal thankfully took the prompt as she placed a trail of soft kisses in a line from Haley's shoulder, along her shoulder blade, and up to her neck.

Haley whimpered at the sensations flooding her system. Her eyes fluttered closed and Cal squeezed her hips more firmly. They popped open again and Cal eased her grip as their eyes met once more. Cal wanted Haley to watch her, that signal was received loud and clear. The thrill of it sent Haley's lust into overdrive and it took every ounce of her willpower not to press back against Cal and search for any contact possible. As torturous as this slow pace was, Haley had a feeling Cal enjoyed being in control, and Haley certainly enjoyed watching her.

Cal placed a few more soft kisses on Haley's neck before she reached her earlobe, a place on her body that Haley had never known was as sensitive as it appeared to be. Haley's legs turned to jelly as Cal sucked on her earlobe lightly before whispering in her ear.

"As much as I love watching your reactions in this mirror, should we move this someplace a little more private?"

The husky tone of Cal's voice held such a depth of desire that Haley was sure she could get lost in it.

"The dorms aren't far, but…I have a small office here too. It's basically just a desk and chair, but it has a lock. It's a cluttered mess, though, so…"

Haley trailed off as Cal ran her fingers under the hem of the thin material of her tank top.

"Closer is better. I don't want to have to take my hands off you to reach the dorms."

Haley gulped as Cal pulled back enough so they could move. Haley turned toward the direction of her office and Cal followed. Her hands remained firmly on Haley's body at all times.

Are we really doing this? How far will it go?

Haley's head filled with a million questions flitting around, which wasn't unusual. Her brain was always full of questions. But right now, Haley didn't care about answers. She wanted to focus on the present, and that meant focusing on the overwhelming sensations her body experienced from Cal's touch.

Haley pushed the door to the office open and stepped through.

"I didn't exaggerate about it being small. There's barely room to move—"

Haley was cut off as Cal pressed her against the wall inside the room and kissed her like she'd never been kissed before. Correction, like she had been kissed only once before. Against a different wall, with the same woman. Haley reached over and twisted the lock on the door until it clicked. Secure in their privacy, Haley wrapped her arms around Cal's shoulders and got lost in the kiss.

It was the type of kiss people wrote songs about, the ones movies faded to black on, the ones books described as mind blowing or all consuming. It was all of those things and more, and Haley could've stayed in this moment forever.

"Fuck, Haley," Cal said as she pulled back. Both of them were breathing heavily and drinking each other in as if it was the first and last time they ever would. The way Cal spoke her name brought an intensity to it, like it was filled with an emotion Haley couldn't place. *Frustration? Anger?*

Something hovering in between them that shouldn't fit within this lust driven moment, but somehow it did.

"Are you going to just stare all day or are you going to fuck me?"

Cal's eyes darkened at Haley's words, and Haley caught the flash of surprise that quickly gave way to pure heat.

"You really are trouble," Cal whispered huskily.

The arousal that dripped from every word emboldened Haley, and some part of her instinctively knew what Cal needed. No hesitance, no uncertainty, no guessing games. Cal needed to know Haley wanted this as badly as she did.

"You keep saying that. Would you like to get in trouble, Cal?" Haley smiled her sweetest smile as she wrapped a hand around to Cal's ass and pulled her closer.

Cal pushed her hand into Haley's hair and kissed her again harder, firmer, sure. Haley nipped at Cal's bottom lip, and Cal pressed a knee between her legs to edge them apart. Haley was still wearing her dance clothes, which meant the tight, thin material of her leggings left very little barrier. Haley's clit throbbed as Cal's knee pressed against it firmly, and Haley groaned into her mouth.

Cal moved her knee and replaced it with her fingers as Haley gasped and dropped her head back against the wall. Cal licked and sucked at her neck as she moved her fingers in a slow, steady rhythm that had Haley aching even more.

"You're so fucking wet I can feel it through your clothes."

Cal spoke the sentences in broken words between kisses, and Haley was sure hearing it made her even wetter.

"You could feel it better without them," Haley panted as she tried to keep the desperation from her voice.

"Is that your way of asking me to get you naked?" Cal asked with a voice far steadier than before.

Haley glanced up at the cool, collected version of Cal that she had danced with so long ago.

"No, it's my way of telling you I want your fingers on me, and my clothes are getting in the way."

Haley wasn't quite sure what had brought this side of Cal back out to play, but she wasn't going to question it. She had a feeling that this was the Cal beneath the person who took care of everyone else. The one who cared about what Cal wanted, and right now, Haley was glad that that Cal wanted her.

Cal leaned in and traced her tongue around Haley's lips as Haley resisted the urge to capture her mouth. Haley wanted to see where Cal would take this, and she was more than happy to follow.

"Just my fingers?" Cal whispered against Haley's lips. Haley's brain was flooded with so many sensations that it took her a moment to understand the question. And once she did, she was flooded with even more.

"I want any part of you on me, Cal. Right now. Please." Haley gave up on hiding her desperation and let the full force of it leak into her words and her face. Cal's eyes widened and her hands moved to rid Haley of her pants without another word.

Cal dropped to her knees and parted Haley's legs with her hands pressed against her thighs. Haley looked down, and the sight that met her was one she wanted etched into her memory forever. Cal on her knees, stroking Haley's bare thighs with tender fingers as she looked back up at Haley. It was the hottest thing Haley had ever seen until Cal reached her tongue out and slowly tasted Haley.

Haley pressed her hands back against the wall to steady herself as Cal pressed her head more firmly between her legs. Cal's mouth explored every inch of her as Haley got lost in the pleasure coursing through every fibre of her body. When Haley thought she couldn't take any more, Cal pressed two fingers inside her and moved her mouth to Haley's clit. She applied a steady pressure with her tongue as she curled her fingers, and Haley saw stars. Bright, twinkling lights bursting through the darkness behind her eyes as a powerful orgasm rippled up her legs and exploded.

Haley's legs finally gave way. As they crumpled, Cal's strong arms were around her, and she lowered them both to the floor in a far more graceful manner than Haley would have managed alone. Haley was straddling Cal's legs, which cushioned her from the bare floor. She blinked her eyes open to find Cal watching her with what almost looked like concern.

"That was intense. I'm not sure I've come standing up before. It made my legs not want to continue working."

Cal broke into a smile that quickly turned into a soft laugh.

"You just say what you think a lot, don't you?"

It was a comment Haley had heard many times before, but there was no hint of judgement in Cal's voice.

"It's not always by choice, but I've learned to embrace that fact about myself," Haley replied.

"I didn't mean it as a bad thing. In fact, I think it's one of my favourite things about you."

Haley's stomach flipped and she smiled.

"You said one. What are your other favourites?" Haley grinned.

"Fishing for compliments, hmm?" Cal joked as she traced soft, slow circles around Haley's lower back.

"Yes, yes I am," Haley replied. Shivers rippled through her body as Cal moved her fingers lower and caressed Haley's ass.

"Right now, you being unabashedly pantsless while we talk is high on my list."

"That seems like a low bar to meet," Haley deadpanned.

Cal chuckled and moved her hand around to the front, slowly making its way beneath Haley's tank top.

"Do you think I often have conversations with half-naked women in my arms?" Cal asked as she expertly unclasped the front clasp of Haley's sports bra.

"I dunno, I mean, the way you did that so quickly does make me wonder," Haley replied. She was joking of course, mostly, but Cal's hand stalled.

"I can promise you, you're the only woman, half naked or otherwise, that I've had in my arms in a long time."

Haley wasn't sure what to reply to that. Why was Cal promising her anything at all? It wasn't her business who or how many people Cal had been with. Except, was it? It had been two years since Cal had heavily implied that she wasn't a relationship person. Things changed in that amount of time. But did Haley want that to have changed?

"You don't need to make me any promises, Cal," Haley replied as she moved her own hand up to cover Cal's.

She moved Cal's hand to her breast, and Cal's eyes flitted closed as she cupped Haley beneath her bra. Haley lifted her top up over her head and stripped off the sports bra before she ran her fingers through Cal's hair.

"Maybe just one promise," Haley whispered as Cal opened her eyes and looked back up at her.

"What?" Cal asked, the huskiness back in her voice.

"I told you before that I don't like regrets. So whatever we do here tonight, or any night this summer, no regrets. Promise me that and it's enough."

Cal was silent for a moment as her face indicated that she was wrestling with her own thoughts. Haley worried she had said too much and broken the spell that had come over them. The one that had let Cal put down her guard and explore the chemistry between them. Haley wasn't ready for that opportunity to be gone, not yet.

"I promise," Cal said before she leaned in and pulled Haley's hardened nipple between her lips.

CHAPTER FOURTEEN

Cal dug her fingers into Haley's ass as she made circles around Haley's nipple with her tongue. There was something so thrilling about remaining fully clothed while Haley was willing and naked in her lap, allowing Cal access to any and every part of her body. Despite the aching throb between her own legs, Cal was enjoying focusing on Haley and kissing the many places she had been dreaming about for weeks. Years even, if she were honest with herself.

Haley had been a recurring star in Cal's dreams, albeit nameless until recently. It was odd to now play those dreams out in real life.

"If you're planning to leave a mark, at least make sure it's somewhere I don't have to explain in my dance clothes," Haley said breathlessly.

Cal chuckled and pulled back.

"Is that your way of telling me I'm being too rough?" Cal asked. She dropped her eyes down to Haley's breasts and noted the red marks of her enthusiasm. None deep enough to mark, though, yet.

"I never used the word *too*. Trust me, if you were doing anything I didn't enjoy, I would say so."

Cal searched Haley's face, and sincerity reflected back at her.

"I'm glad. Because I feel far more comfortable exploring your body if I know you'll let me know what doesn't feel good. Or what does, for that matter."

Haley's fingers were still entangled in Cal's hair. She moved them in circles, almost massaging Cal's scalp in a way that soothed Cal far more than she had realized.

"I don't usually like people playing with my hair," Cal murmured.

Haley went to pull her hand back, but Cal stopped it in its tracks.

"I said usually. You seem to be an exception," Cal said softly.

Haley smiled and continued the circles as Cal stroked the small of her back. Just then, Haley's stomach let out a low grumble. Haley's cheeks pinked up as Cal laughed at the sound.

"That reminds me. I did actually have a reason for coming to see you," Cal said.

"Oh, so you weren't planning to seduce me in front of mirrors and pleasure me in my tiny office?"

The way Haley said things like that so casually made the fire in Cal's body ignite every time.

"Nope. Well, at least not until I watched you dance. Seeing you move so beautifully across the floor in extremely tight clothing might have had something to do with my plans changing."

Haley smiled, and Cal leaned in to press their lips together again. It was an urge she was unable to resist now that she had finally experienced the bliss it brought.

"My actual plan was to make sure you ate. I brought food."

Haley frowned and glanced around them as if Cal had managed to carry the food in unbeknownst to her.

"It's in a bag by the door where I forgot about it because you distracted me. Don't worry, it's not hot food, so it'll still be good."

Haley seemed in no rush to locate the meal, despite her rumbling stomach. She trailed a finger down Cal's body to where Cal's shirt met her pants and edged a line along the seam.

"Well, the cookies were warm, so they probably aren't anymore, but—"

Cal was cut off by Haley's quick movements as she jumped up from her spot on Cal's lap.

"You brought cookies?" Haley said excitedly.

Cal laughed as a still naked Haley stood above her with wide eyes.

"Yes, I did. If you knew about them earlier, would that have changed the trajectory of our evening?" Cal asked as she pulled herself up to a standing position while Haley bounced on the spot.

"I'm not answering that," Haley replied as she batted her eyelids.

"Uh-huh. You get dressed and I'll grab the food. We can go eat by the lake, if you want."

Haley grabbed her pants and pulled them on as Cal headed toward the door.

"But you didn't…"

Haley trailed off, as if unsure how to finish the sentence. Cal stopped in the doorway and turned back.

"I enjoyed myself plenty, Trouble. But right now you need to eat. There's still a whole night left after that."

Haley's face relaxed at that, and Cal went in search of the bag of food she had set by the door on the way in. Had she implied they should spend the night together? Cal's stomach clenched with nerves as she walked toward the door. Instinct had taken over when she had seen the look on Haley's face through the mirror. Haley wanted Cal, and the feeling had been mutual. Cal had pushed her worries aside and let her body do the thinking. Every thought her body had led to exploring Haley's.

There was a difference between losing themselves in a moment and making a conscious choice to continue it, though. If they decided to keep this going later, then it wasn't as simple as a lust-fuelled night of passion. It was something more.

You don't need to make me any promises, Cal.

Haley's words resounded in her head, and Cal wondered where they had come from. Was Haley saying that for Cal, or for herself?

"Are you ever going to tell me where you source the cookies?"

Haley's voice snapped Cal out of her thoughts as she came out of the office. She had dressed and brushed her hair, but the lingering signs of what they had done still remained. Haley's lips were quite clearly well kissed and there were light red marks still fading along her neck. Luckily, the darkness of the night was already setting in outside, and most people were gone to the hall for activities or back to their dorms. But the signs were there, and that was enough to keep the fire inside her fuelled.

"Nope," Cal replied simply as they made their way toward their usual bench. Haley's pout turned to a smile as they sat, and Cal pulled the cookies from the bag. She held them back as Haley reached for them.

"First, sandwich. Then cookies."

"What kind of silly rule is that?" Haley grumbled.

"That's, like, a standard rule. Dessert comes last," Cal said as she placed the bag in Haley's lap.

"But why? If I'm planning to eat them both, what difference does the order in which I do so make?"

Cal considered it for a moment as she dropped the cookies back into the bag.

"I dunno, it's just how things are done. So you don't ruin your appetite and all that shit."

"Well, I've never been very good at doing things just because that's how they're done. If a rule doesn't make sense, then it's not a rule I'm willing to follow."

Haley pulled a cookie back out of the bag and quirked an eyebrow as if daring Cal to stop her. She pulled the soft biscuit apart and popped a piece into her mouth as Cal watched her in amusement.

"I guess I can't argue with that, Trouble," Cal said as she grabbed her own cookie and took a bite.

"What other rules do you defy?" Cal asked as Haley pulled the sandwich out of the bag and unwrapped it.

"Hmmm. I suck at answering questions on the spot because I forget everything. Let me think on it while I eat this. I can't believe you brought me food. Especially food I actually like."

Haley inspected the sandwich and nodded at its contents as if in approval before beginning to eat.

"Do people often bring you food you don't like?" Cal asked jokingly.

Haley finished chewing the first bite of the sandwich.

"Yup. I don't like a lot of textures of foods, so I get things quite plain a lot of the time. People assume if you like certain foods, then you'll eat them together. But I like ham, for example, and I like cheese. But ham and cheese together in a sandwich? No thank you."

Cal was glad she had gone with the plain cheese sandwich, then. She had also gotten a plain ham one that was still in the bag, just in case.

"Well, I've seen you eat lunch a lot and I noticed you usually had plain cheese or plain ham when sandwiches were on offer. So I got both."

Haley stopped chewing for a moment and stared at Cal. Cal's cheeks heated beneath Haley's stare and she squirmed a little in her seat.

"You paid attention to my lunch?" Haley asked after swallowing the bite in her mouth.

"Maybe?" Cal said as she turned her gaze out to the lake, uncomfortable at the attention she had brought to her actions. "Maeve is like that with textures too, so it's something I pay attention to. I know how difficult it can be for her to eat anywhere unfamiliar because of the unknowns that come with other people making your food."

Cal glanced back up, and Haley's eyes were still on her. There was a softness in them that hadn't been there before, and it made Cal's heart flip in a way she tried to ignore.

"You're extremely thoughtful, Cal O'Shea. Don't worry, I'll keep it a secret," Haley said with a grin as she finished off the sandwich. Cal scoffed, but the warmth in her chest grew.

"It's my birthday next week. Can I request more cookies for that?" Haley said as she finished every crumb of her cookie.

"I think that's doable. I'll need to check with my supplier, of course. What day?" Cal asked.

"Friday. So what are we doing?"

Cal made a mental note to remember that.

"For your birthday?" Cal asked.

"No, I meant us, right now. It would be a bit forward of me to assume we'll spend my birthday together," Haley said with a small laugh. There was a hint of nerves in her voice that Cal had a sudden overwhelming need to ease.

"Do you want to? Do something for your birthday, I mean. Unless you have plans."

Cal wasn't sure if she was just trying to avoid answering the original question, or if something else pushed her to ask. Either way, she would've done anything in that moment to see the happy look it brought out on Haley's face.

"I don't have plans. I usually spend my birthday with my mom and Orlaith, my best friend. They know I love my birthday, so they always go all out, but they're probably secretly relieved to get a break this year." Haley laughed.

"Guess I've got big shoes to fill, then," Cal replied as she widened her eyes comically.

"More of those cookies and you've got it down."

They sat in silence for a while as the darkness settled around them. The all-consuming need that sizzled between them had ebbed, and Cal wondered what that would mean for how the rest of the night would go. After her mom had left, Cal had done very little thinking. She had wanted to see Haley, and she had acted on that desire without much thought of where it would lead. But she couldn't spend the rest of the summer acting on whims without considering the consequences, right? So maybe it was time they discussed this thing between them.

"Since you avoided my question about what we're doing, do you want to come back to my room and avoid talking altogether?"

Haley's salacious tone sent shivers through Cal's suddenly alert body, and her clit throbbed in reminder of its neglect. Haley's finger stroked Cal's arm lightly, and Cal stared at her. There was enough light left in the sky to illuminate Haley's face, and Cal was struck by how beautiful she looked sitting on this bench with want written all over her face.

Before Cal had even thought about it, she reached a finger out and stroked Haley's cheek gently. Haley's lips parted slightly, and her features softened as Cal leaned in and kissed her slowly. The worries and fears slipped quietly from Cal's mind as she got lost in Haley's lips.

"Let's go," Cal whispered. They walked hand in hand to Haley's room as a sense of peace Cal had rarely experienced settled over her. She would be damned if she would give that up. Not tonight.

CHAPTER FIFTEEN

Haley woke to an empty bed the next morning, and her traitorous heart sank. It was ridiculous to be disappointed that Cal had left. Haley was the one who had said no promises, and she needed to catch her heart up on that logic. As she picked up her phone to a message from Cal waiting for her, that logic flew out the window altogether.

Hey. Sorry for the disappearing act, but you looked exhausted and I didn't want to wake you. Maeve usually comes to my room before breakfast, so I wanted to be back before she got there, or she would worry.

Haley glanced up at the time displayed in the top right corner. The message had only been sent a few minutes ago. The vibration of her phone was probably what woke her. She caught herself smiling and sighed. What had she gotten herself into? Cal was fun, flirty, exciting. Exactly the type of summer fling Orlaith pushed her to pursue. So why did she have this underlying feeling that this thing between them was so much more than that?

She had an hour to kill before she needed to be at class, so she pressed the call button on her best friend's name.

Orlaith would already be in the studio at this time preparing for her early morning class. She answered on the second ring.

"Hey, traitor. How's camp life?"

"So you're still not over me leaving for the summer, eh?" Haley said with a laugh.

"Nope. But I'll survive."

"Yeah, yeah. I'm sure you're finding other ways to occupy your time."

Orlaith couldn't see Haley wagging her eyebrows, but she was sure her tone implied it anyway.

"Like I'm the only one. From your text updates, your time has been well occupied with your not-so-mysterious stranger. Spill everything."

Haley had updated Orlaith about bumping into Cal and had briefly mentioned they were hanging out a bit but hadn't gone into much detail. Orlaith knew about Cal from that first night in Willow's. It was surreal to Haley now, though, that they were one and the same. The Cal from that night was still shrouded in a mystery that her Cal didn't have.

My Cal. Shit.

Haley would need to work on her categorizations before they got her into trouble.

"She's...oh God, Orls," Haley groaned as she flopped back into her pillow.

"Shit. What's wrong?" Orlaith asked.

The background noises stopped as Orlaith presumably gave the conversation her full attention.

"Nothing. Nothing is wrong. That's the problem."

A beat of silence passed, and Haley pulled herself up to sit cross-legged on the bed as she played with the quilt that sat in her lap. The bedding that still held hints of Cal and what they had done beneath it last night.

"I'm not following. You *want* something to be wrong? Hold up."

Haley pulled the phone back as Orlaith requested to switch to video chat and she accepted the request.

"That's better. Now I can try to make sense of your confusing words by adding in your confusing facial expressions too."

Haley rolled her eyes and leaned back against the pillows to get more comfortable.

"We slept together last night," Haley blurted out, and Orlaith's eyes went comically wide.

"Holy crap. I didn't think you'd actually take my illicit summer fling advice, but go Hales."

"I'd hardly call it illicit. I'm pretty sure there's no rules against two consenting adults getting it on at the camp. Unless it's in my contract and I paid no attention to it, which isn't beyond the realm of possibility."

Orlaith laughed and the phone wobbled slightly as she sat against the studio wall.

"So, let's get back to what's wrong, then. You slept together. And it wasn't good?"

That statement was as far from the truth as one could be. Although good isn't exactly the accurate word for it. It was great, amazing, mind blowing sex. The kind that would pop into Haley's head all day and make her blush at inopportune moments. Like now, for example.

"Your face is telling me it was definitely good. Look at those pink cheeks and that goofy smile. So, good sex. Oh, did she awkwardly disappear after or something?"

Haley's face heated even more and Orlaith winced as if in apology.

"Shit, sorry, Hales. That sucks."

Haley shook her head quickly and tried to gather her thoughts.

"No. I mean yes, but no."

Haley was grateful that Orlaith knew her well enough by now to give her the space to get her words in the right order.

"I woke and she was gone, and I assumed that was what it was. For a split second I was sort of, I don't know, relieved? Like if she just left after sex without saying anything, then it was pretty clear where I stood. But then I checked my phone and she texted and apologized for leaving while I was asleep. She went up to her own room because her sister would be worried if she wasn't there in the morning. It was just…"

"Thoughtful?" Orlaith suggested.

"Yes. That's the problem. Ugh."

"So, you're confused because you had sex with someone you like, it was good sex, and she was thoughtful afterward?"

Orlaith had her head cocked to the side and her eyebrows raised as if she were waiting for the other shoe to drop.

"Well, when you say it like that, it doesn't make sense but it's just…it's less obvious where we stand now. Summer flings aren't supposed to be confusing, right? They are fun sexy times that get left in the past as you leave the camp and each other and they are there to reminisce about in the future."

Haley paused and Orlaith kept up her staring routine before gesturing for Haley to say more.

"But we live quite near each other. It's not like this is a summer fling that can never be anything more because of distance or obstacles in our path."

"Right. So it could be an actual dating situation. And you don't want that option?" Orlaith asked.

"It's not that *I* don't want that option. It's that I get the feeling she isn't the relationship type, and so I don't want to think this is anything more than a fling and end up hurt at the end of it."

"What gives you the impression she isn't the relationship type?" Orlaith said.

"Well, she basically told me so. I mean, it was two years ago, that first night we met, but still. It was pretty obvious she didn't do relationships, and I said there would be no expectations. And then she didn't message me, so that was that. But now there's this."

Orlaith rubbed her forehead with her hand before dropping it to stare at Haley.

"You're basing all of this off a conversation from *two years ago* rather than anything that's been said or discussed right now?"

Haley bit her lip.

"I guess, sort of. She hasn't indicated that anything has changed about that."

"Have you tried, I don't know, *asking* her?"

"Well, sort of. I asked last night what we were doing," Haley said as she picked at the corner of her finger.

"And what did she say?" Orlaith said.

"Well, she didn't exactly reply to that because we were talking about doing something for my birthday. And then, well, we stopped talking because…"

"Because you were too busy ravishing each other until the early hours of the morning?"

Haley's smile gave all the answers needed.

"Okay. I'm not a relationship expert, Hales, but I'm going to try to do the best friend advice thing. It sounds to me like you're still holding on to things from that one night, which makes sense. That night has been your only information about this person for two years. It's hard to let that go and see the person in front of you now. But I think we can both say without question that you are in a very different place to where you were that night. You've grown and accepted things about yourself, and you've *mostly* matured."

Haley stuck her tongue out at that as they both laughed before Orlaith continued.

"Again, *mostly*. But you're assuming Cal is still the same person in the same place in her life as that one brief encounter you two had. How about you go and ask her, and take it from there?"

Haley took a breath and let Orlaith's words sink in.

"Fine. It's just scary. And how do I even know what I want? Let's say she doesn't just want a summer fling. Then I have to actually consider if I want more than that. How do I know?"

Orlaith stared at her for a moment, and Haley stared back as she tried to quash the panic she knew showed on her face. Haley was all too aware that she was spiralling unnecessarily. No relationship, or summer fling for that matter, began with everyone being sure of what they wanted. She should be taking this one step at a time and enjoying everything in the moment. But she also knew that she was prone to jumping in head first, eyes closed. Which often left her wondering how she got from A to Z while the other person was obliviously still deciding if she was a good option.

"If you didn't already know that answer, we wouldn't be having this conversation, Hales. I've got to run now because the class is coming in, but call me later, and try to enjoy yourself. You deserve a bit of fun."

They said goodbye as Haley hopped up from the bed. She was verging on being late, and that was already with skipping breakfast. Time was never something she was good at tracking, and this morning would be no different. After a quick shower, she threw on her clothes and ran toward the gym for her first class of the day.

As she got closer, a figure standing outside the gym had Haley's heart skipping a beat. Not wanting to get her hopes up, she slowed her pace and made her way closer while trying to catch her breath.

"I figured you might need this when I noticed you missed breakfast."

Cal looked a little sheepish as she handed the takeaway coffee cup over to Haley.

"You're my favourite human right now," Haley said as she took a gulp of the coffee and hummed in contentment.

"You're easily pleased," Cal replied with a grin as Haley raised an eyebrow.

"Depends on who's doing the pleasing," Haley said.

"So much trouble," Cal mumbled as Haley glanced toward the gym where the campers were finishing their warm-up with Rowan.

"Thank you for this, seriously. I really have to run because I'm late, but will I see you at dinner later?"

"If you show up," Cal said with a smile and a small wave as Haley turned toward the gym.

"I'll be there. Promise," Haley replied over her shoulder.

"No promises, remember?"

Cal's words made her laugh as Haley turned back at the door to see her walking backward toward the cafeteria. Haley would make it to dinner no matter how many reminders she needed to set. But right now, Cal took up so much of her mind that she doubted she would need any of them.

Chapter Sixteen

Cal's day passed in a flurry of activity. So much so that she was shocked when the dinner staff came in to take over and Ray waved goodbye as they both finished their shift. She hadn't had more than a moment to herself all day, but any spare chance she had gotten had been used for one thing only. Daydreaming about the woman who had just walked through the cafeteria doors.

"You look like your day has been as busy as mine," Cal said as Haley approached.

"It's been a nightmare and I'm starving," Haley replied as they made their way toward the trays. Maeve had eaten earlier with Branna and her friends. They were a good bunch of kids, and Cal was grateful they had easily embraced Maeve into their little group. That meant Cal and Haley would get to enjoy dinner alone. Well, as alone as you can get in a crowded cafeteria with many teenagers and staff.

They found a quiet table in the back corner that was mostly removed from the hustle and bustle of the kids and deposited the food in front of them.

"Did something happen?" Cal asked. Haley had already popped a chip into her mouth and finished chewing before she responded.

"Jace sprained an ankle," Haley said, with stress evident in her tone.

"Jace as in your partner for the finale dance at the end of year show?" Cal clarified, but she already knew the answer by Haley's face.

"The one and only. There's a chance he will be fine by the show, but we've not had nearly enough practice, and I just don't feel like I'll get there in time without it. Obviously, I can practice some of it alone, but the lifts and stuff are a no-go. Rowan is not able to manage them with me, so I think we just need to scrap the whole thing."

Cal chewed her burger for a while and watched Haley. Cal knew how much this finale dance meant to her and how hard she had been working toward it.

"I know it's silly, and obviously Jace resting and healing is far more important. It's just a summer camp show. But I'm sad that the vision I had in my head won't get to happen."

"I could do it with you," Cal said. They both froze, and Cal gulped as Haley's eyes shot to hers.

Where did that come from?

"You would dance with me?" Haley asked quietly.

Cal hadn't danced in a long time. Anytime she had considered going back to it, the reasons she had quit would rear their ugly heads. She always shoved them back down along with any notions of dancing. But the slight glimmer of hope that entered Haley's eyes pushed all of that aside in the moment.

"I mean, not the actual show. But I can help you practice until Jace is back in action. I might not be a good stand-in, but I've had practice with lifts and I'm pretty good at picking choreography up and—"

Haley moved across the table and grabbed Cal's face. She kissed her hard and quick on the lips before sitting back down and grabbing another chip. Cal sat there in stunned silence before glancing around to see if anyone was paying any attention. They weren't, which Cal was grateful for, although she wasn't sure she cared either way. The smile that replaced the stressed look on Haley's face was all Cal focused on.

"Thank you. Seriously. It means a lot that you're even offering. Obviously, I don't know your history with dancing, but I got the feeling it was a touchy subject when it came up," Haley said.

"It is. Mostly with performing, though, so it should be fine since we will only be practicing. I will still need to do my shifts here, but I'm sure I can talk to them about taking some time here and there to rehearse. Plus we can use the evenings."

Haley tilted her head to the side and smiled cheekily.

"Ah, I see, you're only agreeing so you can spend all your free time with me. I get it. If you were that eager you could've just asked, you know."

Cal chuckled while marvelling at Haley's ability to say things like that without care. At least outwardly, that was.

"You've caught me. It's all part of my cunning plan. When do you want to start?"

Haley checked the watch on her hand and Cal finished off the remaining food on her plate.

"How about now? The gym will be empty. I can run through it with you and see how you feel about it. There are some tricky parts, so if you're uncomfortable at any point, just say so. Even the offer still means a lot."

The sincerity shone through Haley's eyes, and Cal gulped. She could get lost in those beautiful eyes all night.

"Who's the eager one now?" Cal said. Haley merely gave a mischievous smile.

"Guilty as charged."

❖

"Okay, I thought I had uncovered your mysterious side and then you go and pull off *that*. What the hell, Cal?"

Cal laughed as she slumped to the floor and gulped water from the bottles they had filled in the cafeteria.

"You knew I danced. It's not that mysterious."

Haley sat cross-legged on the floor across from Cal with an incredulous look on her face. They had done a full run-through of the routine. Cal had fumbled a few parts, but overall it had gone well.

"Lots of people have danced. But not a lot of people can pick up complex choreography in a couple of hours and then run through it like they have been doing it for weeks. Especially people who aren't still dancing every week. I pretty much run a dance studio and I can tell you that *that*"—Haley pointed back toward the floor they had danced on minutes earlier—"was damn near miraculous."

Cal gulped more of her water. She was unsure of what to say and a little unsettled by the buzzing in her limbs. That had felt good. Better than Cal had expected. She hadn't realized how much she had missed dancing until her body started to flow again. It was a reminder of how much it had meant to her once upon a time. Cal hadn't thought about dancing for years to avoid her negative memories, but she hadn't considered that good ones might also surface.

"Tell me to shut up if you want, but I can't help thinking that you've got so much talent, I don't see how any dance coach let you quit. Can I ask why?"

Cal fiddled with the top of her sports cap bottle and wondered what story to give. She could shut it down right now and Haley would let her, Cal knew that. Or she could give a shortened version of losing her teenage passion without getting into the why. Cal glanced up and saw Haley's gaze on her. There was nothing but genuine curiosity in her eyes, and something tugged at Cal. The safety that wrapped itself around her in Haley's presence made her want to be honest.

"Can we go sit on our bench?" Cal asked.

Haley's smile lifted as she agreed. She hopped up to hold a hand out to Cal and pulled her up. Cal stood, and they were face to face with lips mere inches apart from each other. Memories of the night before and what had occurred right there in that gym flashed through Cal's mind. The sudden hunger that appeared in Haley's eyes said that she was thinking the same. Haley leaned in and brushed their lips together softly. Despite the temptation to deepen the kiss and forget about the conversation at hand, Cal didn't. She let Haley pull back and trace soft fingers across her cheek before she dropped her hand back into Cal's.

"Let's go to our bench," Haley said as she turned and led them from the gym.

The way she said *our* had Cal smiling goofily despite the fact that Cal had said it first. There was a slight chill in the air as they sat. The water rippled a little more than most nights with the breeze. They had been lucky with the weather so far for camp, but the sky indicated that was about to change. They sat quietly for a few minutes, and Cal knew it was on her to begin. She kept her gaze trained on the water ahead and took a deep breath.

"I told you a little bit about my mom growing up. She had a rough childhood, and so she didn't have any family. It was just me and her, most of the time. I started dance classes with the local family resource centre when I was a kid, and I loved it. I had a natural talent, and the people there became almost like a second family."

Cal smiled wistfully as the memories of days surrounded by laughter and chat filled her mind.

"My mom wasn't diagnosed with anything when I was a kid. All I knew is that sometimes things would be amazing and other times they would be bad. It could change quickly, so I never knew which to expect. Honestly, I sometimes think if it had been bad all the time, it would've been easier, because I'd at least know what I was in for, you know?"

Haley reached out and placed a hand over Cal's as her voice cracked and she took a minute to shake it off.

"Anyway, the community centre was sort of a safe space where I could be a kid for a while and not care about anything but dancing. Things were in a good place for a while, and I was doing well with dance and my mom used to come to my shows. Which made it that much more noticeable when she stopped."

Cal blinked back tears as the memories she had pushed down so much all came flooding back.

"It usually centred around a guy. She would get a new boyfriend and suddenly he was all she could think about. I would become secondary to that. She would forget to pick me up, forget to have food in the house, forget to come home so I wasn't alone at night. Sometimes I'd get lucky, and she'd pick a guy who wanted to play happy families for a while. Although that usually led to the worst fall-outs when he inevitably left. Mostly, though, she would just stop being my mom until the relationship fell apart and then she would crawl into bed for days or weeks and I would take care of her."

Cal had only intended to talk about why she stopped dancing, but words she had never spoken before tumbled out and she found she couldn't stop them.

"Dance was an escape, until it wasn't. I became numb for years as to whether my mom showed up or not. As a pre-teen it was almost normal not to want your parents there, so I just acted like everyone else who wanted to be cool and independent. Except for me it wasn't really a choice. Then she met someone, and things changed again for a while. He was kind, fun, and caring. He bought me gifts and brought us on trips and came to my shows. They both did. I guess, looking back, he thought being nice to me was a sure way to get to my mom. If only he had known it was an unnecessary effort, maybe I could have avoided getting attached."

Haley squeezed Cal's hand softly.

"He left?"

Cal glanced down and shook her head softly.

"No. Not then at least, but that's what I first thought. It was the night of the last show I did, *Grease*. I was thirteen and had worked so hard on it. I had even been put in a lead dancer role and worked with the choreography for the younger kids. I felt part of something so much bigger than just me or the life I had been used to. I had gotten comfortable because things had been going so well that when the curtain opened, and I saw the two empty seats, I just broke. It was always easier when I expected it to happen, but that time it threw me completely. I left the stage and feigned illness and walked the whole way home alone. I got back expecting my mom to be crying in bed alone, but they were both there in the living room. It looked like they had been arguing, but they barely acknowledged me or the fact that I should've been on stage. I walked upstairs to hide in my room and saw the positive pregnancy test in the bathroom."

"Maeve," Haley whispered softly.

"Yep. My mom had found out she was pregnant and assumed he would be happy since he seemed to love me so much, but the act fell away quite quickly. The arguing continued loudly while I sat in my room, and I heard him talk about how having to deal with one brat just to get in her pants was bad enough, and he didn't want to be burdened with another."

Cal spat the words out as anger rose as clear as it had that long ago night. Anger and heartbreak for a person she had begun to think could be a father to her.

"What a dick," Haley said. It made Cal chuckle lightly.

"That's an understatement," Cal said.

"I hope she showed him the door," Haley said. The words were an echo of Cal's own hopes that night.

"Nope. I understand now that my mom had a deep need to be wanted and loved and tied her value to that. It's something that stemmed from her own less than idyllic childhood. But at the time all I knew was that he said some horrible shit to her about me, and still she begged him to stay."

"Fuck, Cal, that sucks."

Cal was glad for Haley's straightforward commentary that wasn't laden with pity or judgement.

"It did. I hated him from that day. I hated both of them, if I'm honest. And that seeped its way into my feelings about the new baby too. They pretended to be the perfect happy family on the outside, and I felt like the piece that didn't fit. He gave up any pretence of caring about me, and my mom sort of just went along with it. She loved me, I know that, but she cared more about keeping him happy so he would stay. So that she wouldn't be left to raise another baby alone. She kept the peace, even if that meant focusing on him and her new baby and giving me whatever scraps of attention she had energy for once they were happy."

Cal shivered and Haley scooched closer to wrap an arm around her shoulder.

"Anyway, I stopped dancing. I was too embarrassed to go back and too angry to do anything about it. I withdrew from everything and resented my new little sister. One good thing that came from the end of my time with dancing is I realised I loved working with kids. As soon as I could, at eighteen, I took a place in a childcare college course in London and left without looking back. I had little contact with them while I was away. I had a girlfriend and friends and a life that was just about me for a while, and I just wanted to… forget about them."

Cal could hear the guilt in her own voice as the truth slipped out along with the shame it brought her.

"That's understandable," Haley said. Cal pulled back and turned to look at her.

"Understandable that I wanted to forget about my family? That I left my little sister to fend for herself even though I knew what it was like growing up for me?"

Cal spat the words out angrily, but the anger was directed at herself. Haley didn't even flinch as she simply nodded.

"Yes. You didn't leave her to fend for herself, you left her with her parents. The people whose job it was to care for her, even if that was something they hadn't been able to do for you. You had to take care of yourself, and that's what you were doing."

Cal's chest squeezed tightly, and she nodded despite the shame that still cloaked her.

"Eventually, I decided I should visit. I had been gone for almost three years without even a weekend trip home. Maeve had turned seven, and usually Mom would get her to call and thank me for whatever gift I had ordered for her from online, the bare minimum of sisterly duties. But I hadn't heard anything. I realized it had been a while, which wasn't unusual, but I guess I got worried. When I got to the house, it was the middle of the day and Maeve was alone in the living room, in her pyjamas and watching TV. She wouldn't speak to me when I got in and kept staring straight ahead."

Cal vividly recalled the state of the house that day when she walked in. Maeve had clearly been fending for herself for a while, something Cal was all too familiar with.

"My mom was in bed, just sobbing. Maeve's dad had disappeared months beforehand and taken pretty much any money they had. My mom had barely been out of bed in that time except to occasionally get groceries. It was the summer holidays from school, so nobody realized Maeve was basically unsupervised most of the time."

Cal could see the look that came over Haley's face as she imagined the scenario.

"She was seven?" Haley asked softly and Cal nodded.

"I know what you're probably thinking, but my mom wasn't well, you know? She loved Maeve. Just like she loved me. But she was alone, with little to no understanding of mental health and so much shame and trauma. It doesn't make it okay, but she needed help. So I stayed. I took care of them, and we got by."

Haley reached out a hand and cupped Cal's face softly.

"Who took care of you?"

A slow tear slipped down Cal's cheek and Haley brushed it with her thumb.

"I think I'm all talked out for tonight," Cal said with a weak smile as she looked down.

"Stay with me tonight. Let me take care of you," Haley whispered. Cal lifted her eyes to meet Haley's and opened her mouth to reply just as the sky opened up above them and the rain came bucketing down.

CHAPTER SEVENTEEN

Haley ran into her room as Cal followed closely behind. She turned and burst into laughter at the rain dripping from Cal's face. The rain that had stayed away for far longer than usual in Ireland had made up for its absence tenfold. The short journey to the dorms had them both soaked to the skin and shivering.

"I think we should probably get these clothes off," Cal said with chattering teeth.

"I bet you do." Haley grinned as she walked toward the bathroom and flipped on the light switch.

"I'm sure neither of us would be able to stop shaking enough to even attempt to make this sexy right now," Cal replied as she kicked off her shoes.

Haley walked into the bathroom and switched on the shower to let the water heat up. She walked back into the bedroom and pulled her top over her head as Cal struggled to take off a sock. She smothered a laugh as the sock won and Cal landed on her ass on the floor.

"As fun as it is to watch, would you like some help?" Haley asked.

"I am perfectly capable of removing my socks. How in the hell did they get so wet?" Cal said in exasperation.

"Probably due to the canvas shoes with very little protection from the rain."

Cal glowered at her, but the look shifted when she finally noticed Haley was topless and unbuttoning her pants.

"If you stop being stubborn and let me help, we can get into the warm shower sooner," Haley said in her sweetest voice.

Cal straightened her leg and plopped her foot out and Haley peeled the clingy material from it.

"See, all done," Haley said.

She stood back up and dropped her pants to the floor. Her underwear followed as Cal drank in every inch of her body. Haley turned and walked into the bathroom with an extra swish in her step. The heat of Cal's gaze on her back was almost enough to dry her rain slicked skin while it flooded other parts of Haley's body.

Haley put her hand under the shower to test the water. It was a basic standing shower and didn't have a lot of space, but it did come with what looked like a new shower head. The water pressure was surprisingly good, and Haley was grateful for that as she stepped beneath the flow.

"Is there room for us both?"

Cal's voice reached Haley's ears right as hands pressed against her waist.

"It'll be a squeeze but I'm sure we can make it work," Haley murmured as Cal's lips pressed against the small of her neck.

Haley scooted forward to allow Cal enough room to move beneath the water. With firm hands, Cal pressed her body flush against Haley's from behind and Haley hummed in appreciation. The water flowed between them as Haley enjoyed the sensation of Cal's skin against her own. Haley's ass pressed back as Cal moaned and moved her hands around and up Haley's stomach.

"I change my mind about us being able to make this sexy," Cal mumbled against Haley's neck as her hands made their way up to cup Haley's breasts.

Haley chuckled and then gasped as Cal pinched her already hardened nipples. Her body was screaming for more and Haley reached her hand back to grasp at any part of Cal that she could reach. Cal moved her hands to Haley's and spun her around before pressing her against the wall. Haley had a moment to gasp at the cold wall against her back before her gasp turned into a moan of pleasure. Cal's mouth had taken over what her hands had started as she licked and sucked at Haley's nipples. Haley ran her fingers through Cal's hair and pulled her closer.

"Fuck, yes," Haley exclaimed when Cal responded by nipping at her breast with her teeth. The slight sting of pain followed by the immense pleasure that coursed through her stomach almost made her come far too soon.

"Cal," Haley panted as she pulled Cal up toward her.

"Mmm, yes?" Cal murmured. Her eyes were heavy with lust, and the sight had Haley struggling to remember her words.

"Let me take care of you first," Haley said softly as they came back to her. A flash so quick Haley almost missed it crossed Cal's face. Haley wasn't sure if it was confusion or uncertainty, but whatever it was had her reaching up to cup Cal's cheek in her hand.

"Please?" Haley whispered and Cal gulped before nodding her head softly.

Haley stroked her thumb along Cal's cheek for another moment before she switched their positions.

"One sec."

Cal's confusion was clearer that time as Haley stepped out of the shower. She grabbed a fresh washcloth from the pack she kept beneath the sink along with the bottle of body wash. She stepped back into the small cubicle and saw that Cal hadn't moved.

"This okay?" Haley asked, holding up the bottle.

"Uh...for what exactly?" Cal widened her eyes jokingly and Haley laughed.

"I just want to be sure you don't have allergies or anything before I put it on the cloth," Haley clarified with raised eyebrows.

"Oh. Yes. It's just...when you said take care of me..."

Haley wet the cloth and lathered it with the soap as she reached up and placed a soft kiss on Cal's lips.

"Don't worry. I'll be doing that too. But we practiced a lot this evening, and you haven't danced in a while. Your muscles are going to ache in the morning, and this stuff is great at helping them relax."

Cal blinked a couple of times as Haley stepped closer.

"Turn, please."

Cal obliged without question and Haley smiled. There had

been no smart response, no stubbornness, no streak of independence holding her back. For now, even if it was only out of the fact that Cal hadn't been prepared for this, she was letting Haley take care of her.

Haley started with Cal's back. As she ran the cloth along Cal's spine, she used her other hand to massage Cal's tense shoulders.

"Try to relax," Haley whispered.

For a moment she thought this was where Cal hit her agreeable limit. Her shoulders tensed slightly more beneath Haley's fingers before Cal blew out a soft breath and the tension eased. Haley continued moving the cloth along every inch of Cal's exposed skin at her back before nudging her around to face her.

"You're killing me." Cal spoke the words quietly and her eyes were pooled with desire.

"You can tell me to stop," Haley said as she lifted the cloth to Cal's chest and moved it in circles along her skin. Cal didn't respond so Haley kept going. She paid careful attention to each one of Cal's small breasts. Cal's breathing hitched and Haley smiled as she dropped to her knees and pressed Cal's legs apart.

"Haley…" Cal's voice was thick with need as evidenced by the glistening between her legs.

"Are you telling me to stop?" Haley asked as she looked up at Cal while she ran the cloth down her thigh. Cal shook her head softly and Haley ran the cloth back up the other thigh slowly.

"Then let me take care of you."

Haley rinsed the cloth beneath the flow of now lukewarm water before pressing it gently between Cal's legs. Cal whimpered and Haley looked up to meet eyes so wide and vulnerable it made her breath hitch.

"The water is going to go cold soon," Haley said as she dropped the cloth and ran her finger between Cal's legs.

"I don't really care," Cal said as Haley rubbed circles around her clit without getting too close to where Cal ached.

"Mmm, but you will when we're both freezing again," Haley said as she pulled back. Cal let out mumbled protests and Haley chuckled as she stood.

"We're going to get dry first and then I'm going to take care of you the way you assumed I meant in the nice warm bed next door."

Haley hopped out of the cubicle and grabbed two towels. She passed one to Cal and they dried off in silence. Cal dropped the towel into the open laundry basket and ran her fingers through her hair. It was something Haley had seen Cal do in other situations and she had begun to understand it was a nervous habit. They might both be naked, but Cal was raw and uncertain, and Haley needed to fix that.

Haley held out a hand and Cal placed hers in it. She led them into the bedroom and stopped next to the bed. She pulled Cal around to face her and leaned up to kiss her slowly and deeply. Haley manoeuvred their position without breaking the kiss until the back of Cal's thighs hit the bed. She pressed until Cal took the hint and sat down and Haley dropped back to her knees. This time, she had no plans of pulling back before Cal was well and truly taken care of.

Haley spread Cal's legs wide and kissed her way up her thigh. Warmth radiated from Cal, and Haley had to stop herself from rushing to her destination. Cal's hand landed on the back of her head and tried to do it for her, and Haley chuckled softly.

"What happened to letting me take care of you?" Haley said. She looked up at Cal as she placed soft kisses on the uppermost point of her inner thigh and was greeted with utter desperation on Cal's face.

"That's what I'm trying to make happen," Cal all but growled, but the words had a note of pleading in them.

"Your role isn't to make anything happen right now. Just enjoy it when it does. The longer you take to relax, the longer I'll take to get there."

Haley skimmed her lips over Cal's clit and to her other side before placing open mouthed kisses along her thigh.

"Shit," Cal groaned before she inhaled and relaxed back against the bed.

Haley smiled against the soft skin beneath her mouth and flicked her tongue out to trail back up Cal's thigh. She reached up to grip Cal and pulled her forward until her ass was at the edge of the bed.

"I don't love not being able to see you," Cal murmured.

"Mmm, but you can feel me, can't you? Focus on that sensation," Haley replied before pressing her lips to Cal's aching core.

Cal's body melted for her, and Haley moaned her approval against Cal's wetness. Haley wanted nothing more than to spend all night tasting, touching, and pleasuring Cal. Even more than that, though, she had a deep longing to care for her. To wrap her up and protect her from the cruelty of her memories. That longing was far more concerning than the other because it stemmed from somewhere deeper than Haley cared to admit to herself.

"Haley," Cal exclaimed loudly as her legs clamped around Haley's head.

Her body bucked beneath Haley's relentless tongue until she had drawn every last drop of pleasure from Cal. Cal's limbs went weak against the bed, and Haley moved up to join her. There was a depth to the look in Cal's eyes that Haley tried not to read into, but her heart pounded quicker all the same.

What is this? Is now the time to ask?

Haley opened and closed her mouth a couple of times as the words lodged in her throat. So much had been shared between them that night, and Cal looked as raw and exposed as Haley felt. Did that make it the perfect time, or the worst? Cal pulled Haley back on top of her and ran soft fingers up and down her spine as their lips met. They kissed slowly as their bodies rocked together. Haley tried to pour all the wordless questions and feelings from her mouth to Cal's as they came undone together. For tonight at least, that had to be enough.

CHAPTER EIGHTEEN

Cal's eyes fluttered open and for a moment she forgot where she was. The arm slung over her waist reminded her of the evening before and the woman whose bed she had spent the night in. Cal smiled at Haley's sleeping tousled hair, and her heart fluttered softly.

She's so beautiful.

The thought wasn't a new one, but Cal found herself studying Haley's face in a way she hadn't quite allowed herself to yet. She wondered if the light smattering of freckles across her nose was there all year round or only during the summer. She wondered if the barely visible dimple on her cheek had a twin when Haley smiled wide enough. She wanted to know where the small scar above her eyebrow came from. Cal wanted to know everything about Haley, and that terrified her. Almost as much as it terrified her that she wanted Haley to know everything about her.

Cal hadn't spoken the truth to anyone the way she had to Haley on their bench yesterday. Embarrassment, guilt, pain, and mostly shame had kept those things locked up tight. Cal didn't want anyone judging her mom. Her mom held enough shame for her mistakes. Truth be told, Cal didn't want to feel judged, either, for the things that still brought her shame.

Yet despite everything she had shared, Haley had still looked at her with as much longing and desire as before, if not more. She hadn't treated Cal like she was broken or made excuses to cut their evening short after hearing about the baggage Cal carried. Haley had simply taken her back here and shown her what it was like to be taken care of in a way that left Cal feeling both safe and exposed. Cal had no idea how to close it all back up now, or if she even wanted to.

"What time is it?"

Cal startled at the sleepy words Haley spoke before her eyes were even fully open.

"Seven. I need to get going in case Maeve drops by. Although she seems to have ditched me to have breakfast with Branna most mornings anyway."

Haley chuckled and wiped the sleep from her eyes.

"Poor Cal. Well, you're more than welcome to join me for breakfast instead. If I can manage to get there on time today, that is."

Haley stretched, and Cal followed the movements as the blanket shifted to expose the mouth-watering curves beneath.

"Keep stretching like that and there's a good chance you won't," Cal said.

Haley smiled and turned on her side as she tossed the blanket to the side completely.

"I thought you had to go?"

Haley's teasing tone sent shivers down Cal's body as she reached out to cup Haley's soft breast in her palm. Haley's breath hitched slightly as Cal rubbed her thumb in lazy circles around the sensitive skin.

"Mmm, on second thought, she hasn't dropped by in days. And we've got at least thirty minutes before we need to leave for breakfast."

Haley hummed her agreement as Cal moved closer and captured her mouth in a kiss.

"Twenty minutes if you want time to go change first. Our clothes are probably still unwearable since we made no effort to dry them out," Haley murmured in between kisses.

"Twenty minutes is plenty of time," Cal replied as she ran a hand down Haley's body and between her legs.

"You're insatiable," Haley gasped as she parted her legs all too quickly.

"I'm not the only one," Cal replied as her fingers met slick skin before she moved them easily inside Haley.

Cal scooched closer as she pressed two fingers deeper inside. Haley gripped Cal, and a jolt of pleasure shot through her at the slight pinch of Haley's nails digging into her shoulder.

"You make me feel so damn good," Haley panted as she rocked against Cal's palm where it pressed firmly to her clit.

"The feeling is mutual, Trouble."

Haley's eyes locked on Cal's, and Cal's breath caught at the intensity of her stare. It was as if she was searching Cal's eyes for an answer to a question she had yet to ask.

"Is it?" Haley whispered.

The words were barely audible as Cal picked up the pace of her movements.

Their eyes searched each other, and Cal knew the question wasn't only about this moment. Haley wasn't asking about the feelings Cal brought with every thrust of her fingers, or about the building orgasm on the brink of explosion. There was no question between them of whether those physical feelings were mutual.

No, Haley was asking about something they had yet to have a conversation about. Feelings that simmered and swirled between them without being given permission to exist in the space they had unknowingly created since that day in the gym.

Cal opened her mouth to reply. To confirm that yes, of course those feelings were mutual too. Wasn't it obvious in the way her heart beat faster when Haley glanced at her? Or in the way she had watched Haley sleep, simply to marvel at the features that made Cal want to make studying her face a new hobby? Or more important, in the way she wanted to stay in Haley's arms forever and forget that anything else existed?

Forget.

That one word had Cal hesitating a little too long as the loaded silence stretched between them, only broken by their laboured breaths. Before Cal could work up the courage to say any of that, Haley closed the space between them.

Haley kissed Cal deeply, as if absolving her of the need to say anything, and Cal let her. Cal poured the unsaid words into Haley with her lips and her fingers and hoped her body would say all the things she couldn't. It wasn't enough. Cal knew that in the way Haley's gaze didn't quite meet hers as she came undone, and Cal silently begged for her to look again. Surely, if she searched the depths of Cal's eyes, Haley would discover Cal's truth, hidden right beneath the layer of fear Cal couldn't shake. But Cal was sure about one thing, she wanted to leave that fear behind.

❖

"You missed breakfast."

Cal glanced up as Maeve walked out of the dining hall with the kids dispersing to find their first classes of the day.

"Good morning to you too. I'll grab some fruit," Cal replied as she fell into step with her sister.

"Miss Tyne missed breakfast too," Maeve said without a hint of accusation in her voice. But Cal knew all too well that Maeve didn't say things for no reason.

"She misses breakfast most days," Cal replied. It was a truth, if not the whole truth.

"Is she your girlfriend now?" Maeve asked as they neared the building where they would both spend the first half of the morning. Maeve had a drama session while Cal was headed to supervise kids trying to blow stuff up in the name of science.

"Because we both missed breakfast?" Cal joked as she scrambled to think of what to say next.

"You're avoiding the question," Maeve replied in her usual astute way.

They walked quietly for a few more minutes and Cal weighed up how much she wanted to share.

"I am avoiding the question. For a couple of reasons. Partly because I don't have a simple answer, and partly because any answer I do have will require time to explain, and we both need to get to class. Can we talk later?"

Maeve stopped dead in her tracks and Cal scrambled to stop in her stride. She turned back to see Maeve staring at her.

"You keep saying that, but we haven't talked yet. You keep saying it's not simple, but you won't explain it to me. I don't understand why it all has to be so complicated. Either someone is your girlfriend or they're not, right?"

Cal studied Maeve for a moment and took in the hint of frustration in her features. This was about more than their current conversation, and she wondered if something had happened with Maeve and Branna.

"Relationships are complicated things. But I guess the simple answer to your question would be no, we're not. It's not something we've discussed yet."

Yet.

Cal couldn't help wondering if it was something Haley wanted to discuss. Or if Cal did, for that matter.

"Are you putting it off the same way you're putting off talking to me? Because that hasn't been helpful and has just made things more confusing."

Cal took in a breath and pointed toward the low wall beside the building they were about to enter. She moved to sit on it, and Maeve hovered beside her as she quickly checked her watch.

"I'm sorry I haven't explained things well. Do you want to blow off this morning's class and we can go chat?"

Maeve looked at Cal like she had ten heads and sighed dramatically.

"Absolutely not. I've got about two minutes before I need to move again so we won't be late."

Cal laughed and shook her head lightly.

"Okay, little May. We'll talk tonight, I promise. If you don't ditch me for Branna again," Cal said with a grin. The grin slipped as Maeve looked down at her fidgeting hands.

"I don't think that will be a problem."

Cal frowned at the sadness in Maeve's words. What had she missed?

"You okay? We can feign illness and go chat with ice cream."

Maeve looked as if she were considering it for a moment before another shake of her head.

"No, I'm okay. We can talk later. And then you should talk to Haley. I like her, and she makes you smile a lot."

Maeve turned to walk again without waiting for a reply, and Cal fell into step beside her. She would need to make time later to have a proper conversation with Maeve. Cal had been so caught up in this thing with Haley that she hadn't noticed a change with her sister and Branna, and that made the little sliver of guilt poke at her insides again. Cal was due to practice the dance with Haley after lunch, so she would check in with her and see if she had heard anything from Branna. It could help her be a little more prepared for Maeve and the conversation ahead.

Cal noted the way her stomach flipped, and after that morning it was unclear if it was excitement or nerves. She quickly concluded that it was most likely both.

She makes you smile a lot.

Maeve was more perceptive than most people gave her credit for, and she was also right. Not simply about the fact that Haley made Cal smile, but that Cal would need to talk to Haley about more than Maeve and Branna's relationship. With that in mind, the stomach flipping became more nerves than excitement, but strangely enough the excitement remained nonetheless. Cal wanted to avoid a conversation about what they were when she didn't even have an answer for what she wanted, but right now, above all else, she just wanted to see Haley.

CHAPTER NINETEEN

I'm seriously envious of your skills," Haley said as she flopped into a chair in her office. She pointed toward the small fridge in the corner where the water Cal had requested was located and gladly accepted the cold bottle that Cal passed to her.

"Says the professional dance teacher," Cal replied with a laugh.

Haley swallowed a mouthful of cold water and shrugged.

"Exactly. Meaning I am well-positioned to say it. You haven't danced properly in what, over a decade at least? And you're wiping the floor with me out there."

Cal laughed as she leaned back against the desk, and Haley marvelled at how good she looked, even all sweaty and exhausted from their rehearsal.

"We're dancing as partners, so I'm not sure wiping the floor with you is really a good thing. Plus it's completely inaccurate. You're the star in this dance, I'm just there to help you shine."

Cal shot her a cheeky grin as Haley snickered, but her heart fell for that cheesy line nonetheless.

"You already got in my pants, you can cut the charming act, you know."

Haley kept her tone light and teasing and hoped her words would be received as such. Even if part of her was serious about it. Cal's silence that morning when Haley had asked if it was mutual had been answer enough. The look in Cal's eyes left no question of whether she knew what *it* meant, and the lack of response was a response in itself. This thing between them was a summer fling, and

Haley wanted to enjoy it while it lasted. But the more charming Cal was to her, the harder it was to remember all of that.

"You think it's an act?" Cal asked.

Haley's knee was bouncing, and she bit her lip as Cal watched her. There was no hint of teasing in Cal's tone, and she was undoubtedly waiting for a real answer.

"Honestly? No, I don't. Nothing about you seems insincere to me. I just don't think you quite realize how the things you do come across."

Cal's brow furrowed as she considered the statement. Haley jumped up from her seat and began to throw stuff into her duffel bag since it was getting close to dinner time already.

"So, how do they come across?"

Haley startled as Cal's words came from much closer to her than she expected. She turned to find Cal had moved from her perch on the desk and was standing beside her. Haley looked up to meet her eyes and said the first words that came to mind.

"Thoughtful. Considerate. Endearing."

Haley sucked in a breath as Cal's fingers reached out to graze against hers lightly.

"None of those sound like bad things," Cal replied.

"I never said they were bad. They just aren't what I'm used to from someone who just wants—"

"To get in your pants?" Cal finished the sentence as she slid a finger gently across Haley's abdomen and toyed with the waistband of her leggings.

Haley's skin flushed as her body begged for Cal to do just that. Pesky feelings be damned. Who needed to talk about things when being ravished until her body was satiated was an option?

"I'm not complaining. I'm a more-than-willing participant in what we're doing. So feel free to take what you want."

Haley emphasized her point by placing her hand on top of Cal's and sliding both of them farther beneath the stretchy fabric of her pants. Cal closed her eyes briefly before meeting Haley's gaze again.

"What do *you* want?" Cal asked.

She kept her hand still where Haley had manoeuvred it and

made no move to do anything about the throbbing between Haley's legs.

You. All of you. Everything.

Haley searched Cal's eyes for something, anything that would make it easier to lay it all out on the table. She had dipped her toe into it this morning and the result had been disappointment. Albeit short-lived disappointment, as the waves of pleasure from her orgasm had washed it away. Afterward, she had vowed to herself that she would treat this as she had intended. A summer filled with hot, mind blowing sex wasn't something to be upset about, and Haley wasn't going to let it be anything to regret.

No regrets.

That had been Haley's request to Cal, and one she planned to honour herself. Haley lifted her leg and hooked it around Cal. Cal's eyes widened as Haley lifted her hips slightly to press more firmly against Cal's hand as she wrapped her arms around Cal's neck for balance.

"That clear enough?" Haley whispered as she nipped at Cal's earlobe. She pulled back enough to capture Cal's lips with her own in a deep, satisfying kiss. Cal groaned against her mouth before she pushed the thin fabric of Haley's thong to the side and slid two fingers inside her. Haley's responding moan was drowned as Cal kissed her with more desperation than ever.

Cal tugged Haley's other leg up to wrap around her waist. Haley had a moment of worrying that they would fall before Cal pressed her against the desk and gripped her ass tightly from behind. Their new position allowed Cal to press her fingers deeper inside Haley while applying pressure to her clit as it ached for attention. Haley threw her head back and rode Cal's fingers in a steady motion as pressure built in her abdomen.

Haley ran her fingers through Cal's hair as Cal placed kisses along her exposed neck. Cal lightly grazed the sensitive skin with her teeth and Haley pressed against the back of her head to encourage her more. Cal was holding back, and Haley wanted more. She wanted all of the pent up emotions that Cal seemed reluctant to share with anyone, even if it was only in this moment. Cal flicked her tongue out to trace the nape of Haley's neck before she bit down lightly.

It took barely a moment before Haley had to bite her lip to stifle the screams that threatened to erupt. Some part of her was still aware that they weren't exactly in a private place, but right then she cared about nothing but the ripples of pleasure coursing through every inch of her body. Haley clung to Cal tightly and was dimly aware that her nails were going to leave marks. A tiny thrill ran through her at the thought, and she tried to dispel it quickly.

Cal pulled her hand from Haley's pants as she placed soft kisses to her neck while Haley found her breath again. It had been fast and explosive, and Haley wanted more. So much more. She untangled one of her hands from around Cal's neck and toyed with the button on Cal's pants before Cal's hand covered hers.

"I need to go."

There was an apology in Cal's words, and Haley tried to ignore the disappointed pang in her chest. She was well acquainted with the way rejection could overcome her if she wasn't careful, and she couldn't spiral there right now. Not here in the small confines of her office with the person who owed her no promises. She freed her legs from around Cal's waist and slipped off the desk to straighten out her leggings. She would need to go shower and change before dinner which would give her a chance to ride the rejection waves and clear her head.

"Hey, look at me," Cal asked as she reached a hand out to lift Haley's chin.

Haley tried for a smile, but it was weak. No matter how much logic she used or how hard she tried to keep it together until she was alone, unfortunately, RSD didn't care. Logic never played a part in the waves of pain that hit with rejection.

"Trust me, I don't want to go."

Haley wanted to believe that, but her chest still tightened, nonetheless.

"I promised Maeve I would talk to her at dinner tonight. Something's going on with her—she was not herself this morning. Has Branna said anything to you?"

Haley shook her head as she grabbed her bag. Part of her was grateful to Cal for explaining, and the other part wanted to remind her that she didn't owe an explanation. It was like a war between the carefree person she wanted to be and who she was. Someone whose feelings were going to get hurt if she continued down this path.

"No, but honestly, I haven't chatted with her much one-on-one. She's been with her friends a lot and I've been…"

Catching these damn feelings for you.

"Busy with me. Yeah, I feel bad I didn't pick up on something sooner, but Maeve seemed sad earlier when she mentioned Branna, and I need to be there for her. Plus, I keep putting off the conversations she's been starting about relationships and all they entail. I'm not sure my expertise is going to really help her much there."

Cal chuckled lightly as they walked to the door of the gym.

"Maybe she doesn't need expertise. She's a smart and capable kid who might just need honesty from her big sister. I know you worry about getting it all right with her, but maybe she needs you to be her not-so-perfect sister who can relate when life and relationships get messy."

Cal reached out and squeezed Haley's hand gently.

"You're pretty wise, Trouble. Maybe you should enlighten Maeve instead, and me while you're at it. That would be much better."

Cal batted her eyelashes playfully, and Haley didn't have to fake the small smile that grew.

"I'm no expert either. I can barely figure my own feelings out, never mind anyone else's."

Haley wanted to pull the words back in as they were coming out, but it was too late. Cal was looking at her closely, and Haley could practically hear the gears turning as she tried to figure out what to say. Haley knew without a doubt that she was on the emotional edge right now and one wrong word would pull all of her barriers down. Barriers that she needed to keep intact until she was in the privacy of her room.

The intensity of this feeling wouldn't last long; it never did. Haley would need to address this later. She would approach the conversation again when she wasn't liable to react impulsively and ruin any chance of their summer ending on the high they had been riding.

"Speak of the devil," Haley said quickly as she spotted Branna walking toward the dorms ahead of them before Cal got any words out.

"I'll go catch up to her and see if I can get any useful information. I need to shower anyway before dinner, but I'll let you know if it's anything to be concerned about."

Cal hesitated, uncertainty clear in her features, before she nodded.

"Thank you. I appreciate it. See you later maybe?"

The question in Cal's voice held the same hesitance as her face, and both sides of Haley reared their heads to battle again. She wanted nothing more than to spend the night with Cal and continue their all too brief office encounter. But waking up in Cal's arms again while she was already on edge and raw was playing with fire, both in terms of their continued fling and her own heart.

"You should focus on Maeve tonight. I'll see you at the next rehearsal. Bye, Cal."

Haley caught the disappointment on Cal's face and ignored the way it made her want to throw caution to the wind and end the night together again. She turned and jogged to catch up with Branna before she had a chance to do just that. She hoped the distraction of teenage drama would be enough to help her ignore the pull of her heart that was doing its best to drag her right back to Cal's arms.

CHAPTER TWENTY

Cal placed her tray on the table across from Maeve. She had yet to land in the seat before her sister started talking.

"So did you figure out if Miss Tyne is your girlfriend yet?"

Cal had to stop her immediate response of shrugging off the question. For one, this morning was proof that it wouldn't fly with Maeve anyway. And secondly, maybe Haley had been right. Cal was overthinking having the perfect answers for Maeve so much that she had ended up giving no answers at all instead. Maeve was obviously frustrated by Cal's continued dodging of the conversation, and it wasn't protecting her to ignore things either. Cal didn't have all of the answers to Maeve's questions, but maybe it was time she trusted that what she did know was enough.

"No, I didn't. I like spending time with her, but I'm not sure that I want a girlfriend right now, does that make sense?"

Maeve pushed food around her plate.

"What's up, little May? Talk to me," Cal prompted gently.

"It doesn't make sense. But that's sort of what I said to Branna, too."

Cal waited a moment, and when nothing followed it, she noticed Maeve glancing around the cafeteria nervously.

"Hey, how about we grab these to go and eat outside instead?" Cal asked.

Maeve looked relieved and Cal hurried up to grab some containers and a bag. She set about wrapping up their food and they walked the short distance to some picnic benches scattered around near the cafeteria. They were full of people during lunch time breaks but were always less crowded for dinner time. Cal was glad to find them empty as they grabbed one farther back from the courtyard. She pulled the food from the bag and set it up.

"Okay. So what did you mean by that's what you said to Branna?" Cal asked.

"Well, I like spending time with her a lot. She's fun and kind and beautiful and she makes me feel happy. I think about her lots, and I want to spend a lot of time with her and that's why I was asking you those questions. Because I didn't understand how I should know the difference between if it's because I like being her friend, or because I want to be her girlfriend."

Cal waited as Maeve paused to take a drink.

"That makes sense. I know I didn't do great at answering that, but I promise to do my best to be honest and help you figure it out if that's what you want."

"Well, Branna told me that she liked me as more than a friend. And she sort of asked me if I wanted to be her girlfriend."

Cal slowly chewed the bite of food she had taken and tried to moderate her reply. Internally, she flip-flopped between *oh my God, no, you're a baby* and *oh my God, my sister's first girlfriend*. She swallowed the bite and went for a more neutral response.

"How did you feel about that?"

She would thank her therapist later for that line.

"Well, I told her that I didn't know if I wanted a girlfriend right now. Like you said about Haley."

Cal winced. Hearing her own words reflected back from Maeve was a stark reminder of the influence she had on her sister's impressionable mind.

"Was she upset? Even so, it's okay to not say yes if you're unsure. It's hard to do but it's important to think of what's best for you."

"Well, it wasn't really the truth, though. She makes me happy, and I like her a lot, and it is different from with my other friends. So when factoring all of that in, I know that I do want to be her girlfriend. It would be illogical not to want to be when I am happier with her than I am without her. But I got scared when she asked me, and it sort of came out."

Cal suppressed a smile at Maeve's logical rundown of her feelings.

"You're way too self-aware, you know that? It's okay to get scared too, this is all new territory. Can you tell her that?"

Maeve started to push her food around again and Cal waited patiently for her to consider the question.

"She didn't react badly or anything, but I could tell she was hurt, and I've barely seen her since. We had different groups and I've been sort of avoiding her for meals and I miss her. But I don't know what to do."

Cal reached out a hand slowly and let Maeve finish the distance before she squeezed her hand softly.

"You need to talk to her. Tell her what you told me. That you were scared, and this is all new for you, and you realize now that you do like her the same way. If she's worth your time, kiddo, she'll understand."

Cal's phone lit up from where it sat face up on the bench and she glanced down at it. Her stomach flipped when she saw Haley's name on the screen.

"Is that what you're going to do?" Maeve asked as she gestured toward the phone. "Talk to Haley instead of being too scared and hiding?"

Cal clicked into the message and ignored Maeve for a moment as she read the text on the screen.

Talked to Branna. She says Maeve is avoiding her because she asked her out. She wants to let Maeve know that she misses her friend, and she wants that back. Shared this with her permission because she asked me to get Maeve's number from you so she can text her.

"Why doesn't Branna have your number?"

Maeve looked confused before Cal flipped the phone around and showed her the message. A soft smile grew on Maeve's face as she read the words. It was adorable to watch her sister navigate her first romance, even if it did make Cal feel like the years were passing all too quickly.

"Because my phone is for emergencies, and I didn't see a reason why Branna would need me in an emergency."

Cal stared at Maeve, who looked right back as if it made perfect sense.

"Hold up. You only use your phone for emergencies?" Cal clarified.

"Yeah. When you gave it to me you said it was for emergencies. It only has your number, Mom's, and the emergency services."

Oh boy. Cal was usually careful with the rules she gave Maeve. She could often follow rules too precisely, and Cal had missed the mark with this one.

"Maeve, that was almost two years ago. I didn't mean you could never use it for anything else. How do you talk to your friends? Or google shit to find answers?"

Maeve seemed completely unbothered by the situation.

"I talk to my friends every day at school. I have my tablet to google things or there are also these things called books that hold a lot of information."

Cal rolled her eyes as she mumbled, "Smartass," under her breath.

"I would've asked you if I wanted to use the phone for anything else, but there hasn't really been a need yet."

Cal began tapping out a response to Haley as she listened to Maeve.

"Well, there is a need now. You're going to want a way to keep in touch with your girlfriend when we get home."

Cal glanced up and Maeve's smile was still in place. She was grateful that Maeve's relationship issues were far more easily resolved than her own.

"She said she wants to be friends," Maeve said.

"She said that because she thinks it's what you want. And she values you enough to put her own bruised ego aside and keep your friendship if you don't want any more. Which makes her a good person in my books. So tell her how you really feel and trust yourself to make the right decision for you."

Maeve looked scared, and as much as Cal wanted to wrap her up and protect her from all the dangers in the world, the excitement that mixed with the fear stopped her. Cal never wanted Maeve to get hurt and she knew all too well how much first loves could hurt. But that was the kind of stuff Maeve should be experiencing. The kind that came with first kisses and first dates and lifelong memories that mended broken hearts.

There were some things that Maeve had to endure that Cal would erase in a second if she could. But the smile that lit Maeve's face as her phone chimed mere minutes after Cal had shared her number was something she would never take away from her.

"Branna wants to know if I'll go to the movie with her later. She said just as friends."

Maeve looked panicked and elated all at once and Cal chuckled.

"Go. And ask her if it can be a date instead. That's what you want, right?"

Maeve nodded in response but made no move to reply to the message. Her eyes scanned the screen as if decoding the words for meaning.

"Look at me, little May," Cal said as she plucked the phone from Maeve's grasp.

Maeve looked up, and Cal was once again struck by the difference a few weeks had made to her sister. She had always been wise for her years, a fact Cal knew didn't come without learning too many lessons too soon. But as Maeve sat there looking nervous and excited and full of feelings she was still trying to understand, she looked exactly the age she was.

"If you tell me you're not ready to date, then I will help you find a way to say that kindly and you can keep being Branna's friend. That's okay to decide. You're my favourite person in the whole world and I want you to be happy. Any person would be lucky to get to be your first date, and if that person isn't Branna, that's okay. But what I don't want is for you to be afraid to make any decision at all and years from now wonder what would've happened if you had just pushed past that fear. I don't want you to have any regrets. So tell me, do you want your first date to be with Branna?"

Cal wasn't asking the question for any clarity for herself. The answer was already written all over Maeve's face. She was asking to give Maeve the time to see it for herself.

"Yes, I do."

Cal began to type a reply on Maeve's phone.

"Wait, what are you saying?"

Maeve didn't sound concerned which warmed Cal a little more than she expected. She wasn't worried that Cal would say something she didn't like because she trusted Cal and that meant everything.

"I'm helping you along a little. I haven't sent it yet, so you can read it and delete anything you don't like. Only send it when you're ready to. But sometimes, people just need someone to help them make that start."

Cal handed the phone back and Maeve read the short message as Cal gathered their containers into the bag to dispose of. The movie was being shown on a projector inside the hall at eight, which was approximately an hour and a half from now. Maeve wouldn't want to be late, and this was her little sister's first date. Cal wanted to make sure it was one she would add to the good memories pile that Cal hoped would soon outweigh the bad.

"Okay, I sent it. I need to get ready."

Maeve hopped up before she checked the time and Cal knew she was calculating how long she had to do just that.

"Come with me. We're going to go get you ready for your first date and you're going to gush about Branna and all the reasons she deserves the honour of being your first girlfriend."

Maeve fell into step beside Cal as they walked toward the dorms.

"You've met Branna, remember?"

Cal laughed and shoved Maeve lightly before ruffling her hair in the clichéd, big-sisterly way she loved.

"Yes, yes. But I'm pretty sure I don't know the same Branna that *you* do," Cal said with a wink. She laughed at the pink that crept its way onto Maeve's face.

"You know I haven't forgotten you're still avoiding the topic of you and Miss Tyne, right? Maybe you should take out your own phone and type the same message you typed on mine. Or do you wanna be wondering years from now what would've happened if you'd pushed past the fear?"

Maeve smiled, clearly proud of herself for using Cal's own words against her.

"Things get a tad more complicated when you're an adult, so enjoy it while you can," Cal joked.

"Is it really more complicated, or do adults just complicate things unnecessarily to avoid facing their fears?"

Cal wanted to tell Maeve all the ways that it wasn't that simple. But her far too wise sister wouldn't accept that answer, and Cal knew Maeve would be right.

CHAPTER TWENTY-ONE

"You realize this is the first year in like over a decade that I won't be planning your birthday celebrations, right?"

Haley could practically hear the pout in Orlaith's voice as she popped the phone on speaker so she could continue getting ready for the day.

"Yes, yes, I know. You should be thankful you're off the hook this time. Plus, we didn't celebrate *on* my birthday every year. So we can do something when I'm back. I am totally good with extending my birthday celebrations for you."

"You're not back for, like, more than a whole week. Celebrating it a night or two later is different to a couple of weeks," Orlaith replied grumpily.

"You sound like a toddler on the verge of a tantrum. You realize my birthday is supposed to be about *me*, right?"

Haley threw on her favourite hoodie and wrapped her arms around herself to revel in the cosy familiarity. She needed comfort today, and there was nothing quite like an oversized, out of shape piece of clothing to offer exactly that.

"Fine. You make some sense. So are you going to celebrate with your, what do we call her now, *friend*?" Orlaith asked.

"I have no idea. That was the plan, but then things got weird. Plus I only actually mentioned it once, so I don't know if it was a serious plan or not."

Haley hadn't spoken to Cal much since her awkward goodbye outside the studio. Apart from the two of them playing middlemen for Maeve and Branna, they had yet to have an actual conversation. Preparations for the end of year show were well and truly underway, so they were both run off their feet with excited teenagers and rehearsals. They weren't due to practice the dance until Saturday, which would be their last run-through since Jace was due back next week. So Haley had no obvious excuse to demand Cal's time or attention to talk. Or to do anything else for that matter, which Haley was acutely missing already.

"Weird in what way? Did you talk to her about how you were feeling and how she might or might not also feel?"

Did I?

Haley kept replaying it in her head, and she was still unclear about it all. She had been so sure that Cal was brushing her off, but as she got some separation from the situation and her heightened fear of rejection, she began to wonder if that was the truth. Had she even given Cal a chance to reply? Or maybe she had, and this was her desperate attempt to cling to the remnants of hope.

"Sort of. She made some comment about feelings being mutual and I used that as an opening to ask if they were and, well, she didn't really reply. So I feel like I need to take that as an answer."

Haley sank into her hoodie a little more and was grateful for the small things that helped her regulate her emotions.

"She just said nothing? Like, did she change the subject noticeably or was there an awkward brush-off?" Orlaith asked with confusion in her tone.

"Well, not exactly. We were in bed and sort of mid…"

Orlaith's groan rang through the speaker and Haley could picture the exasperation on her face.

"You're telling me you tried to talk about feelings mid-sex? And that seemed like the most opportune moment to you?"

Haley had asked herself the same thing a number of times since, but she still needed to justify it to Orlaith.

"I didn't exactly plan it that way. It just happened. But even so, I feel like if she were interested in more, then I'd know that by now. I'm not getting that from her. I don't think I can put myself out there any more than I already have, Orls."

Orlaith sighed and Haley picked the phone up so she could get going to class. She grabbed her medication and swallowed it with some water before searching for the bag she left packed by the door.

"I don't like the idea of her using you for sex and you getting your feelings hurt," Orlaith said.

"That's not what's happening. Cal has never been deceptive or pursued me and strung me along. If anything, the opposite is true. I'm the one who made it quite clear I wanted to sleep with her. And plus, isn't using someone for sex exactly what you told *me* to do this summer?"

Haley held the phone between her ear and shoulder as she locked the door to her room. She grabbed a protein bar from the stash she always kept in the front of her bag as she headed toward the gym. It would have to do as her breakfast since once again, she'd failed to judge time accurately. Haley used to wish she could be more prepared and get to places on time, but she had come to terms with the fact that that would never be part of her skill set.

Being prepared in Haley's book now meant preparing for the reality of her time keeping skills, or lack thereof. It was much easier to prepare for the person you were than the person you thought you needed to be. If keeping a stash of protein bars eliminated the cycle of trying to make breakfast, failing, and feeling bad about it as well as hungry, then it was what she would do.

"Yes, well, you wouldn't have been hurting my best friend's feelings in the process, so that was different."

Haley swallowed the bite of the cookies and cream protein bar in her mouth and laughed softly.

"Ah yes, who cares about other people's feelings, eh? Thank you for the concern, but I knew what I was getting into. I'm a big girl, Orls, if my feelings get hurt it's on no one but me."

Haley checked the time and took another bite as she hurried her steps.

"Well, was the sex at least worth it?" Orlaith asked in a hushed voice. Orlaith was already at the studio and likely only in a semi-private area, which Haley hoped did not contain her mother.

"God, yes," Haley answered without hesitation.

Orlaith chuckled softly and they stayed on the phone in companionable silence as Haley neared the gym.

If nothing else came from this summer with Cal, there was no doubt in Haley's mind that she still wouldn't change the past few weeks. Hurt feelings and potentially even a bruised heart were a price Haley was willing to pay for everything she had gained this summer. Not just amazing sex, which in itself was an experience worth the sacrifice. But Haley got to see parts of Cal that she was sure nobody else ever had. She got to be the person Cal opened up to about things she had been carrying around for far too long, and that was an honour Haley didn't take lightly.

"Even if nothing else happens, I'm glad I put myself out there this summer. I don't regret any of it, Orls, so don't worry. I have class now, so gotta run. Talk soon?"

"It's your birthday tomorrow. So duh. Text me later if you want to talk through the feelings stuff more, you know, if you're not busy ignoring it because of the hot sex."

Haley laughed and ended the call as she greeted the full-of-energy kids waiting to practice for their part in the upcoming performance. The show would take place on the last day of camp so that family and friends coming to collect the kids would get to watch. It would be a mismatched display of talent, creativity, and passion, and Haley was excited to see it all.

They would begin proper onstage rehearsals most evenings next week, so the hall would be set up from Monday on, and Haley couldn't wait to see all of the kids' hard work come together. As with any school-like shows, there was a wide variety of talent on display, but Haley loved how the show was specifically designed to give everyone their time to shine, in whatever way they were most comfortable with.

"Miss Tyne, can I talk to you for a minute?"

Haley turned to find Maeve fidgeting behind her and smiled genuinely. They had grown close over the past few weeks, and not only because of Haley's connection with Cal, or Maeve's with Branna. Maeve clearly had some of her sister's talent with dance, albeit not as much of Cal's natural confidence while performing, but Haley had loved seeing her flourish from class to class as she relaxed into herself and her body.

"Of course. What's up?"

Rowan was nearing the end of the warm-up, but they would be fine to start the class without her. Haley would be sure to give Rowan the glowing recommendation they deserved from this camp and was excited at the future they had ahead of them in this line of work.

"Branna told me about your dance studio, and I wondered if I could talk to you sometime about seeing if I could go when we get home. I don't know what the classes cost, but I have some savings from birthdays and I just…I really like dancing in your class."

Haley had an overwhelming urge to hug Maeve but settled for a smile that she hoped conveyed the sincerity of her gratitude.

"I love hearing that you're enjoying it. You should definitely be in a dance class, and I would be honoured if you chose to come to mine. We will work something out, but I expect to see you at my first class of the semester, bright and early."

Maeve's lips curved in a smile.

"I'm always up early, so that works for me. Thanks, Miss Tyne."

Haley had given up on telling Maeve to call her by her first name. It wasn't going to happen in the confines of the class, and it was more than a little endearing. She was grateful for her mom's sliding scale fees, but she would've made it work for Maeve no matter what. One of the perks of being the daughter of the owner meant she had a little freedom with that kind of thing.

"Oh, by the way, I'm supposed to subtly find out what your favourite type of cake is. Branna didn't know the answer, and I have no clue how else I would be able to find that out subtly, so could you just tell me instead?"

Haley laughed as warmth spread through her at the question. Cal still remembered her birthday. At least, that's the only assumption she had as to why Maeve would need to find that out.

If not, Haley was in for a big disappointment, but she let her hopes stay up regardless. Cal didn't seem like the type to forget something like that.

"Hmmm, that's a hard one. I like most types of cake that don't have too much going on. If I were to pick one favourite, I would say chocolate fudge."

Maeve took in the information as if it were part of an important mission and then headed back to the class without another word. At least one thing was for sure, there was cake on her horizon, and that fact alone was enough to make Haley start her first class of the day with a smile.

Chapter Twenty-two

Cal glanced around and bit her lip nervously.

Is it too much? Is it enough?

She was way out of her depth here. Knowing she was up against a lifetime of what sounded like amazing birthdays from other people who loved Haley too, and knew her far better than Cal did, was a little bit terrifying.

Hold up. Love Haley too?

Cal balked at her own thoughts and shook herself. If everything went to plan, Haley would be there in less than three minutes. And since Maeve was the one in charge of making that happen, they would be exactly on time. There was no time to waste questioning herself about a slip of the tongue. Although, did it really count as a slip of the tongue if it wasn't uttered out loud?

"What is all of this?"

Cal spun around quickly and her heart beat loudly in her ears. She had gotten distracted and forgot to keep a look out for them, and now here they were. Haley was standing in front of her in a denim jumpsuit that looked like it was designed for her.

"Wow."

The pink that crept up Haley's cheeks made Cal aware that she had spoken aloud. The sun was framing her face in a beautiful golden glow, and Cal couldn't have contained the utterance if she'd tried.

"Ahem. We are on time, right?" Maeve waved her hands as she spoke.

Cal looked at Maeve and Branna as they stood awkwardly to the side, and she rushed to get back on track.

"Yeah, uh, yes. You are. You're always on time, little May."

Cal kept her eyes on her sister for a moment to slow down her heart rate and gather her thoughts.

"What is this?" Haley asked again in little more than a whisper.

"It's your birthday celebration," Maeve filled in for her while Cal continued trying to pick her jaw up off the floor.

What the hell is happening?

Cal couldn't pretend that Haley didn't affect her in more ways than physically. Their connection had been clear from the first dance they shared two years ago, and it was still there when they stood in the gym for the first time weeks ago. But the feelings that were zipping through her nervous system right now were more intense than anything Cal had experienced before, and she had no idea what caused it.

Well, that wasn't wholly true. She had some ideas. The beautiful woman standing before her with a goofy, excitable, and slightly confused look on her face, for one.

"Sorry, I got distracted and forgot the time," Cal said as she gestured for them to sit.

"I'm the queen of that, so no worries," Haley said as she sat on the mismatched blankets laid out upon the floor.

"We're having a picnic?" Haley asked with a smile.

Cal was more nervous than the situation called for as she sat down across from Haley. "Yep. Picnic for four, complete with deli made sandwiches, *fresh* fruit, and of course the highly requested triple chocolate chip cookies."

Cal laughed as Haley went straight for the cookie and took a bite.

"You're supposed to have your sandwich first. Cookies are dessert," Maeve said as she frowned at Haley.

"I wouldn't get into it, kiddo. You won't win this one," Cal said as Haley laughed. Maeve looked horrified as Branna grabbed a cookie too.

"Live a little," Branna said as she wagged her eyebrows and

held the cookie out to Maeve. Cal was a mixture of amused and freaked out. She wasn't quite sure seeing her sister being fed a cookie by her girlfriend was quite in the realm of her comfort levels yet, but she had nothing to fear.

"I am living just fine, thank you. I'll have my cookie *after* I finish my sandwich."

Cal laughed and was proud of the fact that her sister would be unlikely to cave to peer pressure, even while clearly smitten. It was also clear that Branna adored that fact about Maeve by the look on her face in response.

"How'd you get those banners to stay up?" Haley asked as she glanced around them.

With great difficulty.

"Oh you know, just a little twine on the branches," Cal said as she downplayed the effort it had taken to decorate outdoors. Although it was a nice summer's day, it was still Ireland, and the ever present fear of rain made her idea seem terrible. But the look on Haley's face as she took in their surroundings was worth every moment of Cal's tortuous setup.

She had picked this spot a little off to the side of the large green area where people lounged between classes. It was close enough to see the lake, but far enough that the sounds of activities were a distant background noise. There were trees around them, and Cal had decorated them all with banners, balloons, and even some streamers made by Maeve and Branna in art class.

"She started setting up like three hours ago," Maeve said, and Cal glared at her. Maeve glanced up and frowned at Cal's stare.

"Was I not supposed to say that?"

Haley's smile grew wider, and she chuckled softly as Cal's face heated.

They ate their picnic in between conversation, laughter, and some light music that Cal put on her phone to drown out noise from some of the more enthusiastic water sports taking place on the lake.

As they neared the end of the food, Cal jumped up to rummage through the bag she had placed behind the tree. She fumbled with the matches she had borrowed from the campfire kits and cursed as the third one failed to light the candles placed on the small chocolate cake.

"Need some help over there?" Haley asked as Cal's profanities got louder.

"No, I got it," Cal replied in a far more confident tone than she felt. She most certainly did not have it, at all.

"Let me do it," Haley said, and Cal jumped as a hand landed on her shoulder.

"You can't light your own birthday candles. That's just sad," Cal said as Haley plucked the matches from her grasp.

"You should know by now that I'm not good with following arbitrary rules. Plus, you're likely to start a forest fire if someone doesn't take over." Haley chuckled.

Cal stood up and held the cake in front of her as she glared over her shoulder.

"You'd think maybe one of the two other participants who *aren't* celebrating their birthday would offer."

"They are clearly far too busy making googly eyes at each other," Haley said, as she struck the match on the first try and lit the candles with ease.

"I swear you used different matches or something," Cal mumbled, as she nudged Haley to go back and sit down. Haley grinned as Cal pressed play on the song waiting on her phone. "Happy Birthday" played softly as she walked toward them slowly with the cake and hoped the candles would stay lit for the short journey.

"Make a wish," Cal said as she placed the cake in front of Haley.

Haley glanced up at her with the most beautiful look on her face before she blew the candles out to cheers.

"What'd you wish for?" Branna asked, as Cal pulled the candles from the cake and produced a knife for Haley to make the first slice.

"She can't tell you. That's not how wishes work," Maeve said as she nudged Branna lightly.

Cal found herself wishing that this was one of those arbitrary rules Haley would ignore. She was disappointed when Haley agreed with Maeve and kept her wish to herself. Cal wanted more than anything right now to reach inside Haley's head and find out what she wished for herself. Was it something Cal could help make come true? It was a ridiculous notion, but Cal had a sudden, intense desire to do just that, for this and every wish Haley had.

"We gotta get going," Branna said as she and Maeve jumped up from the blankets.

It was their lunch break right now, and they still had an afternoon of activities to attend. Haley had the afternoon off, and Cal had taken the day off herself to make all of this happen. They waved them off, and Haley turned to Cal with a gentle smile.

"Thank you for this. I know it must have been a lot of effort, and I loved it."

Cal was packing the remnants of their picnic into the bag as they got ready to go.

"It's not over yet. We're going to go eat your cake on our bench and then continue the birthday celebrations," Cal said as she carefully packed the cake back into its box.

"There's more?" Haley said with wide eyes.

"Well, it's your birth*day*, not birth*hour*, right?" Cal joked.

Haley laughed, but the soft look in her eyes had Cal melting in all the right places. She busied herself with ensuring there was no trace left behind in their picnic spot before they walked toward their bench overlooking the lake. It was less peaceful at this time, with the water sports ongoing, than at night. But they ate their cake while laughing at the inexperienced kids losing their balance and hoped they were far enough away to not be caught making fun of them.

"We're going to hell for that one, you know that, right?"

Cal's shoulders shook from laughter as she tried to stop long enough to respond.

"Come on, not even a so-called saint could've held it in with that. He was bragging so much and then splat."

Cal wiped tears of laughter from the corner of her eye as she mimicked the action.

"Plus, he was being a dick to the girl ahead of him, so I don't even feel a tiny bit bad."

"Good point," Haley replied as she finished the last bite from her slice of cake. Cal popped the paper plates in the rubbish bin beside the bench before she checked the time.

"Okay, let's get going," Cal said as she picked up the bag of picnic supplies and gestured for Haley to join her.

"Where exactly are we going?" Haley asked as she fell into step beside Cal.

"This way," Cal said as she pointed them toward one of the buildings beside the hall.

She led them to a room right at the back of the building that she had commandeered for the afternoon. She pushed open the door and was glad to see nothing had changed from when she had set it up that morning.

"I was hoping to use the hall since it was already set up from movie night, but there's karate there later, and I didn't want to have to rush. Plus, it's a much bigger place to make look pretty. So I borrowed the projector instead."

Haley was looking around with her mouth open in what Cal took as a good sign. She had hung string lights around the walls of the room to allow a soft glow of light that wouldn't impact the visibility of the movie being projected onto the clean whiteboard. Cal had chosen this room partly due to its distance from any camp activities for the day, and also because it was bare of tables apart from a couple placed against the wall. She had lined the floor with as many blankets and pillows as she could get her hands on that morning as well as a couple of bean bags to give plenty of seating options.

"You did all of this?" Haley asked quietly.

"Most of it. Maeve and Branna helped with securing some of the blankets and pillows from the spares in the dorms and helped me gather enough lights. I will need to return some of them tomorrow before onstage rehearsals for the show, but nobody will miss them today."

Cal's heart began to pound in her chest again at the way Haley looked at her then.

"This is what I meant." Haley looked as if her words were spoken without her permission.

"Meant?" Cal asked as she walked toward the projector and loaded up the movie.

She needed to keep her eyes away from Haley for a moment or they would end up forgetting about the movie altogether. The opening credits of *Dirty Dancing* filled the screen, and she turned back to find Haley still stood in the same spot. The music from "Big Girls Don't Cry" began to play, and it snapped Haley out of whatever trance she had been in.

"Never mind. Let's watch. But you know I'm going to want to practice the dance after seeing it here," Haley said with a laugh as she plopped into one of the oversized bean bags.

"Your wish is my command," Cal replied as she threw herself onto the other bean bag and focused on the movie.

CHAPTER TWENTY-THREE

Haley pinched herself several times throughout the movie, but nope, she was awake. And had fallen smack dab in the middle of her very own unrealistic romance movie, it seemed. The juxtaposition between this and the assumptions she had made the past week about the continuation of their situation was stark. After Maeve's not so subtle questioning yesterday, it was obvious that Cal would keep her plans to celebrate Haley's birthday with her. Haley assumed that this was out of duty rather than desire considering she had sort of thrust it upon Cal by bringing up her birthday.

She had spent the past few days convincing herself that she was completely fine with this thing between them continuing, and ending, as a hot summer fling. That the high was worth the inevitable low that would come at the end of camp. If Haley kept her expectations in check, it would be bearable. It would be worth it, and her bruised heart would recover just fine.

Then Cal went and did *this*. She not only celebrated Haley's birthday with her, but put hours of time, effort, and thought into organizing several components to the day. And suddenly all of Haley's understanding about their situation and her acceptance of the future were thrown on the proverbial fire and blown to pieces.

"You okay?"

Haley blinked a couple of times as the end credits of the movie rolled. Cal was looking at her with concern.

Am I okay?

She turned to look at Cal directly as Cal's eyes flicked to

Haley's lips and back up again. There was an undeniable hunger in their depths despite the concern clouding her features.

This woman isn't going to bruise my heart, she's going to damn well break it.

Haley reached out a hand to cup Cal's cheek and ran her thumb along the soft skin.

"Thank you for this," she whispered, and Cal visibly gulped.

"It's your birthday," Cal said as if that were explanation enough.

Haley leaned in and pressed their lips together in a kiss that held none of their usual intensity or even passion. It was simple, sweet, and soft. Precious. That was the word that resonated the most, and Haley made no move to push it further or pull away.

Words might not have passed Cal's lips when they discussed feelings, but Haley was beginning to see that words weren't everything. If Haley considered things without the lens of her own fears in the way, it was obvious. Cal had shown Haley time and again that she thought about her, cared about her, had feelings for her. That was no longer in question, not after today. Whether Cal was willing to do anything about those feelings or not would be the question, but right now, Haley didn't need answers. She only needed Cal.

"I had planned for us to go back to our bench in a little while and have dinner. I even found those folding TV dinner tables to use and…"

Haley kissed Cal again as tears pricked the corner of her eyes in gratitude.

"That sounds amazing. It really does. And I don't want to waste any of the effort you've gone to, but…"

Haley pulled back a little and searched Cal's eyes in the hopes of conveying what she wanted.

"But?" Cal asked.

Haley knew the question wasn't out of uncertainty because she had no doubt Cal understood what she meant. It was another moment of Cal giving Haley an opportunity to be sure, and she was.

"But I need you to come back to my room now and celebrate with me in my bed," Haley stated.

Cal's eyes widened and she blew out a soft breath as her lips curved in a smile.

"I love when you say exactly what you're thinking," Cal said as she stood and pulled Haley with her.

They made their way back to Haley's room quickly and were barely through the door before Cal had her pressed back against it.

"You sure this is how you want to spend the rest of your birthday?" Cal asked in a teasing tone as she pressed a hand beneath Haley's top and cupped her over her bra.

"Well, not just this. But here is a start. We can end it in the bed."

"Fuck," Cal murmured as she slipped her hand beneath Haley's bra.

"Precisely," Haley replied with a grin that was quickly cut off by a moan as Cal's finger and thumb worked her aching nipple.

❖

"So have you always wanted to teach dance? Or was it a falling into the family business kind of thing?"

Haley turned her head to face Cal as she considered her answer. Hours had passed since they returned to the room, and they were still naked in Haley's bed, giving their bodies time to recover from the exertion.

"Well, I was in college for dance, and most of my peers were pursuing the professional dancer route. My mom wanted that for me too, and for a while I sort of just went along with it. Then my mom's studio struggled for a bit financially when people were less inclined to fork out for things that seemed like luxuries to most, like dance classes."

Haley remembered how hard it was to even get her mom to admit they were having issues. It had been obvious to Haley for a while, but her mom tried to make it work until Haley took it out of her hands.

"My mom was trying to keep on top of it all. She built that studio from the ground up and she didn't want to hand any part of the reins over to anyone else. But teaching dance and running a business including marketing and accounts are different skill sets. And my mom was always keen to keep costs low, so it was affordable for people. She had grown up without the money for extracurriculars and always says how she owes her whole career to the local community centre and the dance teacher who only charged what people could afford."

Cal hummed in agreement.

"I get that, I mean I felt the same about the community centre I got to attend. Looking back, I'm sure my mom missed payments constantly for the classes I attended, but I was never made to feel any different to anyone else there. But I can also see how it's not an easy way to run a business and make a living."

"Exactly. Don't get me wrong, I adore that about my mother and I'm glad I got those traits from her, too. I don't ever want money to be a barrier to someone finding their love of dance. But there had to be a balance, and my mom wasn't the one to be objective enough to find it. So I finally convinced her to hire a studio manager. He was a guy I went to college with, so he was happy to take on the role at a very reasonable rate since it was great experience for him. He had an eye for creating opportunities to get people into the studio, and made my mom see how charging more for the people who could afford to pay was the key to keeping costs low for those who needed that. Anyway, I took on more classes at the time to help offset the cost, but now the studio is in a great place. I can do anything I want without worrying about the studio, and I am. Hence the summer volunteering here," Haley said.

"So you never wanted to go professional?" Cal asked.

"Well, I mean, I wouldn't say never. When I was younger and watching dancers in shows on stage, I thought maybe that's what I wanted to do. It was certainly what everyone told me I should aim for. Especially my mom," Haley replied as she played with the hem of the light sheet that was covering her body.

"I've seen you dance, so I'm not surprised people also saw that potential and wanted you to use those talents to their full extent," Cal said.

Haley had heard that one before so many times. Her mom had always dreamt of Haley becoming a professional dancer. It was a dream that stemmed from one her mom had for herself once upon a time, before she wound up a single mother and followed a different path. Her mother didn't fully understand Haley choosing to follow the same path when there were other options available.

"See, I understand why you think that professional dancing is using my talents to their full extent. But I disagree. If I danced professionally, then I might have the potential to affect some people in an audience for a night who enjoy my performance, right?"

Cal turned to look at Haley as she continued.

"Teaching means I get to affect people every day. I get to help make dance beautiful and accessible to so many children in ways it isn't always, like with you and my mom. I know you understand the potential in that. And who knows, maybe some of those kids will go on to perform night after night to audiences who get to watch them shine because I helped them see they could."

Cal reached out her hand and entwined her fingers with Haley's.

"I hadn't quite thought of it that way, but that makes sense. I guess I wondered if you stayed to help your mom with the studio and maybe gave up on fulfilling your own dreams for that."

Haley's skin tingled at the soft strokes of Cal's thumb over her hand.

"I couldn't dream of anything more fulfilling than using my talent in a way that builds up others and shapes a community. It's a powerful way to live, and one I admire my mother for every day. Look at this camp and the way the kids have flourished week on week. Getting to be a part of making that happen is beautiful, don't you think?"

Cal leaned over and kissed Haley briefly.

"I think you see the world in a way everyone should, and that is what's beautiful."

Haley's cheeks heated and she had to resist the urge to pull the sheet up to hide from the intensity of the moment and Cal's stare.

"It was my birthday, you know," Haley said quietly.

"It still is your birthday," Cal said with a confused smile.

"No, I mean that night. The first night we met in Willow's when we kissed and then you ghosted me," Haley said. She added a smile to soften her words. "It was my birthday. So technically we met two years ago tonight."

Cal's face seemed to drain of colour and Haley frowned.

"You okay?" Haley asked.

She'd thought mentioning it would be a nice moment for them to reflect on, but the air shifted in a way she hadn't foreseen.

"That night was exactly two years ago?" Cal asked in a quiet voice.

"Yeah, it was. I was just kidding about the ghosting stuff, you know that right?" Haley said.

"I need to check on Maeve," Cal said.

The change of topic caught Haley off guard. Cal was patting the bed around her as if looking for something and then pulled her phone from the bedside locker.

"Shit. I need to go," Cal said as she jumped out of the bed and looked around for her clothes.

"Is this a joke?" Haley asked hesitantly. If so, it wasn't a funny one, but she had no idea what else could've changed in the last minute.

"It's Maeve," Cal said as she began frantically pulling clothes on, and Haley sat up in concern.

"What's wrong? Did something happen?"

Cal was pulling her shoes on and gave no indication that she had even heard Haley speak.

"Cal, stop. Talk to me. What the hell is going on?"

Cal stopped for a moment and looked at Haley like she had forgotten she was even there. There was a brief flicker of something on her face.

Fear? Anger? Regret?

But it was gone before Haley could discern it, and in its place was something else. It was as if the caring, vulnerable, open Cal she had spent the day with was gone and in her place was the Cal that had walked off the dance floor and away from her that night.

"If you walk away from me again without even telling me why, I'm not following you this time," Haley stated.

It sounded harsh even to her own ears. Maeve was important to Cal, and Haley respected that. If something was going on with her, then Haley would never ask Cal to stay and ignore it. She had proven as much when she had woken to an empty bed the first night they slept together. At least Cal had given her a clear reason in her text message then, and Haley had no issue with her wanting to be there for Maeve. But Cal was also an adult with the ability to communicate. Haley deserved more than two words. She deserved more than to be an afterthought in her mind, to be left scrambling to figure out what went wrong when the only person who could tell her was choosing not to.

"I'm sorry," whispered Cal, before her eyes went back to her phone and she walked out the door.

Happy fucking birthday to me.

CHAPTER TWENTY-FOUR

"You're overreacting."

Cal paced the small room as she tried to calm her racing thoughts and heart.

"I'm reacting. There's nothing *over* about it."

Maeve huffed and Cal resented the sound. She had yet to take a deep breath since seeing the numerous missed calls on her phone from both Maeve and her mom when she'd checked it earlier at Haley's.

Haley. Fuck.

Cal had a moment of deep shame before she was distracted by Maeve again.

"You're making me dizzy, can you at least sit down?"

Cal stopped her pacing and dropped into the chair at the side of the sole treatment bed in the makeshift nurses office at the camp.

"What the hell were you thinking?" Cal asked as she eyed the bandaged arm strapped to Maeve's chest.

"I was thinking it was a calculated risk and the odds were on my side. Unfortunately, odds aren't guarantees," Maeve stated.

Cal put her head in her hands and willed herself to calm down. Logically, she understood that her reaction was more about the places where her mind had gone when she saw those calls, rather than the reality of the situation. When Haley had mentioned it being two years ago that they met, Cal had gotten a sickening déjà vu feeling. She was instantly reminded that it was two years since she had lost track of time and left her sister alone with their unconscious mother.

She had tried to find the words to explain why to Haley, and to remind herself that things were different now, but the missed calls on her phone had sent her into a tailspin. How often before had Cal thought things were different only to end up devastated all over again? How often had she let her guard down and let her focus slip from her family, only for them to wind up hurt?

"Your arm is broken. That doesn't sound like a calculated risk to me," Cal finally replied.

"Technically, we don't know that it's broken yet. They need to X-ray it for that. The chances of breaking my arm on a skateboard are surprisingly not that high. Plus, concussion poses the biggest risk to skateboarding and I wore a helmet, so we don't have to worry about that."

Cal looked up from her hands as Maeve shrugged nonchalantly and wanted to shake her if that wouldn't injure her further.

"Listen. I know I told you I wanted you to have experiences here. And I'm not opposed to you trying a skateboard for the first time. But deciding that first time would be on a *rocky hill* without *any* adults present was not what I had in mind. I bet you didn't put those facts into your calculations because I'm pretty sure that would raise those odds. Were you trying to impress Branna?"

Maeve looked a little offended by the suggestion, and Cal almost laughed. *Almost.*

"No, Branna told me not to do it actually. But I watched some YouTube videos first and I wanted to know what it was like. She's a little mad at me, I think. She yelled at her friend who let me try his board," Maeve said sheepishly.

"She's probably more scared than mad, which I can relate to. Although I am definitely mad. You can't learn everything from YouTube, little May. Especially when it's related to something that could wind up with broken bones or concussions."

"I wore a helmet," Maeve repeated, but stopped there when Cal glared.

"And I appreciate Branna looking out for you, but this isn't her friend's fault. You made the choice to take it from him."

Maeve nodded in agreement.

"I told her that. I didn't just take it, I asked for it. He was a little unsure, but I told him about the odds."

Cal closed her eyes and took a deep breath. As air filled her lungs, her heart finally began to steady its rhythm.

"You're not making me less mad, little May," Cal said.

"I wasn't trying to. I'm telling the truth. Is Mom on the way?"

Cal glanced at the time on her phone. It had been over an hour since she managed to get onto her mom to find out that the nurse had called her when Maeve couldn't get through to Cal. When the line had first connected and Cal had heard her mom's voice, even and steady, she had collapsed onto the step outside the dorm room buildings and sobbed. Her mom had spoken softly, calmly, as if understanding exactly what Cal had feared.

Cal had sobbed in a way she had never allowed herself to for her mother. Her mom had waited until Cal gathered herself to finally let her know that Maeve was in the nurse's office and needed an adult with her so they could make a plan to bring her to the hospital for an X-ray. The nurse was thankfully understanding of Maeve's resistance to being touched and had gently gotten around her to treat the wound as best she could when Cal arrived.

Their mom was already on the road when Cal had gotten back to her, so it made sense for them to wait for her to drive them to the hospital rather than someone from camp making the journey. Maeve was comfortable enough with the painkillers she had been given to wait, and she would feel better in their mom's familiar car than anywhere else.

"She should be here soon, little May."

"Good. She can bring me to the hospital, and you can go back to celebrating Haley's birthday. Did you finish dinner yet?"

Cal's stomach churned uncomfortably, and she avoided looking at Maeve.

"I'm coming with you," Cal said.

"But there's no point in that. You'll just be sitting in the waiting room."

"I'm not leaving you go alone," Cal said with finality.

"I won't be alone. I'll have Mom," Maeve said, and Cal flinched unconsciously.

Something about hearing those words from Maeve irked Cal in a way she couldn't quite explain. Was it because Cal wanted to be the one to be there for Maeve? Or was it because Cal had never been able to say the same thing with such surety? There was no time in her life that Cal could remember being able to rely on her mom to be there for her without question. If she wasn't giving her all to a new relationship, she was recovering from the last one. Cal had seen her mom lose herself in relationship after relationship, which had left Cal alone at the times she needed someone the most.

Kind of like this evening when Cal had lost herself in Haley and almost left her sister alone with a broken arm. Part of Cal understood it was an irrational comparison to make. Maeve was okay and had never been totally alone. But she couldn't help the niggling feeling that lodged itself in her gut. That this was another reminder that Cal didn't have the luxury of allowing herself to relax with someone else without risking her world falling apart in her absence.

"Well, look at the ruckus you've caused, kiddo. You doing okay?"

Cal looked up when her mom walked into the room and toward them. She was looking at Maeve but made her way to Cal and squeezed her shoulder tightly.

"I'm okay. I tried skateboarding," Maeve said, and their mom laughed lightly.

"Well, I'm glad you're trying new things, kiddo. Next time maybe give us a heads up first."

"That's sort of what Cal said, but madder," Maeve said.

Cal looked up as her mom moved her arm from where it squeezed Cal's shoulder to place it around her more firmly. Cal dropped her head against her mom's side where she stood next to the chair. Exhaustion enveloped her as the events, both real and imagined, of the night caught up with her. Her body was still alert and ready to react to the danger it had been anticipating, but her mind was completely and utterly drained.

Her mom kept her arm around Cal and rubbed her back in soft circles in a way that Cal hadn't remembered forgetting about. She had flashes of the same thing from when she was a child, and her body responded by relaxing as if it had been waiting for permission to do so. Cal wasn't sure when the soothing gestures had stopped before, but from the look on her mom's face, Cal knew that part was her doing. As a child, she had pulled away from her mom in more ways than one for self-preservation, but maybe when things had calmed down, it would be time to work some of that out once and for all.

SYNCHRONICITY

CHAPTER TWENTY-FIVE

*C*an *we talk?*
      Haley stared at the text on her phone before locking the screen again. Days ago, that message would've at the very least given her some semblance of relief, but now it was too little, too late. When Cal had walked out of her room with nothing but an apology, Haley had lain in bed and cried until she couldn't cry anymore. What had started as one of the best birthdays she could remember had ended with her as a sobbing mess pouring her heart out to Orlaith on the phone.

Her best friend had made her promise that enough was enough, and she would keep the remnants of her heart intact until she got home and they could work through things properly. Haley had heard from Branna about Maeve's accident and hospital trip, so Cal's frenzied exit made a smidge more sense. She understood that Cal likely saw a message about Maeve being hurt and with her overprotective big sister hat on wanted to rush to be with her.

But did that really require not saying a word of explanation to Haley? Even if Cal had been in shock in the moment for some reason, didn't Haley deserve a message of apology or explanation sometime between then and now? Days had passed and Haley kept expecting her phone to light up with Cal's name, or for Cal to seek her out at camp, but neither had happened. Instead, Haley felt like an afterthought, only worthy of her time when Cal decided so.

Haley was okay with being nothing more than a summer fling,

because that, she had signed up for. What she was absolutely not okay with was being made to feel like she wasn't worthy of respect.

"I'm sorry about the dance," Rowan said as they tidied up after another long afternoon of rehearsals.

"No worries. It wasn't meant to be this time. There's always next year," Haley said lightly with more forced nonchalance than she would've liked.

Jace's ankle wasn't at full strength yet and it was too risky to do the end of year dance. A fact that Haley understood and wholeheartedly agreed with, but which saddened her immensely. More than she wanted to admit to anyone the way she had to Cal. It was an end of camp show, and it was about the kids, not her. But Haley was proud of the choreography she had put so much time and effort into and was sad that it was another disappointment to take away from her summer.

"You're back!"

Haley turned when she heard the excited exclamation from one of the kids. It was quickly echoed by the rest of the group as Maeve walked through the gym doors sporting a crisp white cast on her arm. Maeve walked farther into the gym as choruses of her peers asking to sign the cast surrounded her.

"Okay, okay, how about we give the girl some space, eh?" Haley said as Maeve smiled at her in gratitude.

"Hi, Miss Tyne," Maeve said quietly as she got toward the stage where Haley was gathering things at the side.

"Sorry I ruined your birthday and that I can't dance in the show."

Haley stopped what she was doing to focus fully on Maeve.

"You absolutely did not ruin my birthday. And you can most certainly dance in the show if you're still up for it, but it's also fine if you don't want to."

Maeve looked at her in confusion as she held up the cast as if Haley had potentially missed it.

"But I have a cast now, so I can't do the moves like we practiced," Maeve said, matter-of-factly.

"Then I guess we'll need to adapt those moves, eh? We can

figure it out in rehearsal tomorrow, but I would be sad if you missed the show because of that. You've worked hard. Maybe if you practice as much on a skateboard, you might stay on it next time," Haley said.

Maeve smiled brightly at that.

"Cal says I'm never allowed on a skateboard again, but she's dramatic. I think she was more scared than mad, like she said Branna was."

Haley's heart hurt at the mention of Cal. She tried to keep her face neutral because it wasn't her place to talk about any of that with Maeve.

"I bet she was. Branna is gone for lunch and I'm sure she'll be very excited to see you back. Did you have to stay in the hospital?" Haley asked.

"I know. Branna texted me earlier, so I'm going to meet her in the cafeteria soon. I wanted to let you know *we're* back first"— Maeve emphasized the plural, and Haley understood the real meaning behind her coming here—"and nope, I was only in the hospital until the cast was done. We stayed in the hotel near the hospital for a couple of nights. Cal wanted us to go home, and then her and my mom were arguing and stuff, and eventually I told Cal she could go home if she wanted, but I was coming back here."

Haley nodded and said her goodbyes to Maeve as she left in search of Branna. Her heart was heavy with the knowledge that Cal had thought not to return at all. In fact, she had probably only contacted Haley today because she would have to see her again. If they had gone home without returning, would Haley have ever heard from her again?

It solidified Haley's choice to not respond and to put Cal, and the memories both good and bad, to the back of her mind. When she was home in the safety of her own environment, she could pull them back out and sort through them properly, including savouring the parts she would want to remember. But for the sake of getting through the last few days of camp with some of her dignity, and heart, intact, she needed to focus on the show and the reasons she had come here to begin with.

❖

"Maeve says she's miserable, you know," Branna said.

"I'm sorry to hear that," Haley said as she shifted uncomfortably on the bench. The sun was high in the sky today, and the warmth felt good on her skin. She had successfully avoided Cal since her return to camp, apart from some awkward glances across the busy cafeteria. Anytime Cal had seemed to be making her way toward her, Haley had become engrossed in conversation or found something she needed to go do.

"If you were sorry, then you'd talk to her," Branna replied.

"I'm busy. Plus, that's none of your business and she shouldn't be putting you in the middle of it."

Branna exaggeratedly rolled her eyes in the way teenagers did best.

"She's not. She won't even talk to Maeve about it. But we both have eyes and can see what's going on. You're both miserable because of whatever happened on your birthday that neither of you will talk about. Even though you *both* told Maeve and me to talk to each other when we were being ridiculous, and that worked out well."

Haley had no idea how to get Branna to understand without divulging things she shouldn't hear. So she would need to be okay with being the bad guy here if that's what needed to happen.

"I'm glad it worked out for you two, you're adorable together. But that isn't the way it works for everyone, okay? You're right, something happened on my birthday, and it upset me. I know that Cal is upset that I'm not talking to her about it now, but I need to focus on the show and my job here. Even if I'm not dancing in it anymore, I'm still choreographing the whole thing, and that's a lot of work. So that is my priority and I need you to respect that, okay?"

Branna tilted her head before shaking it slowly.

"Nope. I won't respect it because it doesn't make sense. The show is tomorrow, and then camp ends. So, then what? Will you have another excuse? Sounds to me like you're just avoiding your feelings, and that's not the Haley Tyne I know and admire."

Haley was speechless at the teenager spouting life advice at her and getting it far too on point.

"You admire me?" Haley teased since it was the only safe part of the statement she could reply to.

"I'm beginning to question that," Branna deadpanned before her eyes flicked to something behind her and a smile lit up her face.

There was only one reason for that, and Haley's heart pounded as she glared at Branna, hoping against hope she hadn't done what Haley suspected she had done.

"Oh, crap, I forgot I promised Maeve I'd go to the movie with her since it's the last one of camp. I'll see you later."

Branna hopped up and waved cheerily as Haley stared daggers at her. Cal took the seat Branna had vacated and waved awkwardly.

"She didn't tell you I was coming, did she?" Cal asked as she pointed to where Branna and Maeve were making their great escape. They were giggling and glancing back like they had successfully re-enacted *The Parent Trap*.

"Nope. Did Maeve tell you?" Haley asked.

They were here now, and Haley didn't have it in her to get up and walk away. What harm could it do to talk a little and then leave without it being a scene?

"Yeah, she's not much of a liar. She left out the part about you not knowing I'd be coming, though. I can go," Cal said, but she made no attempt to leave.

"It's fine. I can't stay long anyway. I need to go make sure everything is set before the show tomorrow."

Haley had yet to look at Cal properly. She finally raised her eyes and regretted it instantaneously. The shutters were still well and truly in place. Cal was here, but the vulnerability was gone, and it made Haley want to take back her previous statement and tell her to go.

"I'm sorry for how I left the other night," Cal said. So they were going straight into it, then. Haley appreciated that—she hated tiptoeing around a subject, even if she would've rather avoided it altogether.

"Yeah, it was shitty to have no clue why. But I know now it was because Maeve was hurt. I would've understood if you'd have just said that, though," Haley replied.

Cal glanced down and then back up, and Haley could've sworn she witnessed those shutters waver in her eyes.

"That wasn't why," Cal said. Haley furrowed her brow in confusion but stayed silent. If Cal wanted to talk, she could talk. Haley wasn't going to drag anything out of her.

"When we met two years ago, I did have every intention of messaging you when I got home. I know I implied at the time that I didn't want anything more, but I felt..."

Cal trailed off as if searching for the right words. Haley wanted to interrupt and tell her to stop. She had no interest in rehashing all of it, and Cal didn't owe her an explanation for two years ago. She owed her one for now.

"I felt a connection with you, and I thought that maybe it was one I could explore."

Haley raised her eyebrows at that. It wasn't what she had expected to hear and if anything, it made her more confused.

"I thought maybe things were finally settled enough for me to take some time for me, you know? So I was going to text you and ask you out. Then I got home, walked into the living room, and saw my mom passed out on the couch. She had overdosed, and Maeve was alone with her, rocking in the corner. I had let my guard down and lost track of time, and my sister had to sit alone and scared. My mom almost died."

Haley's heart sank as Cal's voice cracked. She wanted to reach out and cover Cal's hand with hers, offer some form of comfort, but she was unsure how it would be received. And right now, she couldn't handle it if Cal pulled away.

"I'm sorry. I didn't know."

Cal's eyes were glazed, as if reliving a night that must've etched itself into her brain.

"When we were in your bed, and you mentioned that it was your birthday..."

Oh no.

Haley had unknowingly reminded Cal that it was not only her birthday, but the anniversary of that night too.

"I wanted to explain, to tell you why I pulled away when you said it. But then I looked at my phone and I had all these missed calls from Maeve and from my mom. I just panicked, I couldn't think straight."

It all made far more sense to Haley now with that missing piece of context. Another thing Haley had taken away from therapy was that trauma, and the effects of it, weren't linear. One trigger could rip a healing wound right open and make you feel the effects of that moment again in full force. Not only had it been the anniversary of a clearly significant trauma for Cal, but seeing missed calls from the people involved in that trauma must have been overwhelming.

"I'm sorry, Cal. That must've been terrifying. I wish I had known so I could've helped you, rather than the way it ended up going. If I had known—"

"You have nothing to apologize for. I didn't tell you, so how could you have known? But maybe it was a good thing that it happened. It was another reminder of why I can't..." Cal trailed off and her eyes darted anywhere but at Haley.

"You can't what?" Haley asked, while already knowing the answer. It was written all over Cal's face.

"I can't be in a relationship. I know we've never officially called it that, but...we both know it's where it was heading. I love spending time with you, and this summer has been amazing. It was the perfect distraction, but I can't afford to be distracted anymore. My family needs me, and I can't risk..."

Cal trailed off again, and Haley let the silence envelop them for a few moments. Her heart pleaded for her to try and change Cal's mind. But the little voice in her head reminded her how it felt to be the one always chasing, always begging for more, never being enough to fight for.

"I meant it when I told you not to make me any promises. Bar one, remember?"

Cal looked up and Haley had to brace herself against an onslaught of emotion at the sadness in her eyes. Regardless of what happened, this was still somebody that Haley cared about, and she hated to see Cal in pain. It would be almost easier if Haley could think that Cal didn't have feelings for her. The idea that it was one sided and nothing more would be an easier loss to work through than the loss of so much potential right here in front of them.

"No regrets," Cal whispered softly.

"No regrets. I'm not going to try to change your mind, Cal. For my own sake, I can't do that. I understand you have things to work through, but I also know I deserve someone who thinks I'm worth the risk."

Cal opened her mouth as if to protest and Haley held a hand up to stop her.

"Let me finish, please. Telling me I am worth it when you're not willing to prove that won't help. But I do hope that you find a way to work through those barriers and decide someday that *you* are worth the risk. That *you* deserve more. So that when the next person comes along and you charm them off their feet, you'll be in a place to see it through. Your family is important, Cal, but so are you. Remember that."

Haley stood then and wiped a stray tear from her eye. She would let the rest fall in the safety of her room while wrapped in her cosy hoodie.

"I wish things were different," Cal said. She stood awkwardly, as if unsure whether to walk with Haley or stay.

"Don't wish for things you're not ready to get, Cal. I'm going to go now. Can you wait a little, so we don't do the awkward walking in the same direction thing?" Haley attempted a light laugh, but the tears lodged in her throat made it difficult. A ghost of a smile crossed Cal's face as she nodded in response.

"Bye, Cal," Haley said. She turned and walked quickly away with the certainty that she was leaving a piece of her heart behind.

CHAPTER TWENTY-SIX

Cal woke up with a headache pounding behind her still closed eyes. It was a painful reminder of the fact that she had spent most of the night crying and far too little of it sleeping. Cal wasn't usually a crier, but everyone had their breaking point. Hers was apparently the image of the woman she loved walking away from her with nobody for Cal to blame but herself.

The woman I love.

Was that who Haley was? Cal's heart leapt to attention in enthusiastic agreement. Four weeks was entirely too little time to be feeling that way, but hearts didn't care about things like that. If Cal had to pinpoint exactly when this began, though, she would have to look farther back than four weeks. Love at first sight wasn't something within the realm of Cal's usual beliefs, but the undeniable connection between them had been evident two whole years ago.

Even the mere fact that Cal had been drawn to Haley at the bar while on her way out the door had to indicate something, didn't it? Not that it mattered now. Cal was doing nothing more than torturing herself with questions about feelings she couldn't pursue, regardless. Haley had been more understanding than Cal deserved yesterday, and it was yet another reminder of why Cal had to take this step back.

Haley was right when she had said she deserved someone who thought she was worth the risk. Haley deserved someone who could give her the time and attention a new, blossoming relationship needed. Not someone who was still waiting for the moment her life got blown up again, when she would need to pick up the jagged pieces like she had so many times before.

"You're still in bed?"

Cal blinked open her eyes and winced at the light as Maeve flicked the switch on.

"What time is it?" Cal asked hoarsely.

Her throat was dry and gritty. She sat up in search of the water bottle she kept on her nightstand.

"It's eight o'clock. You look terrible."

"Gee, thanks. Love you too," Cal muttered as she took a gulp of the room temperature water.

"What does loving me have to do with how you look?" Maeve asked as Cal swung her legs around to stand. She had painkillers in a bag somewhere, she was sure of it.

"I didn't sleep well, and my head is banging. I packed some ibuprofen, but I have no idea where it is."

Maeve opened the bag she had over her shoulder and pulled a mini first aid kit from it. Of course she had a mini first aid kit in her bag. Cal would never be as prepared as her sister even if her life depended on it.

"I'm not surprised, your room is a mess. You know we're leaving today, so that means you need to pack. Rooms need to be vacated before the show, so bags need to go to Mom's car when she arrives, which is in two hours."

Cal took the painkillers that Maeve held out and gulped them down with the water.

"None of that is helping my headache," Cal mumbled as she walked to the bathroom to splash water on her face.

"I've already had breakfast with Branna before I came to check on you. So if you want to go eat, I'll start your packing," Maeve offered.

Cal popped her head back around the bathroom door.

"You will? Have I mentioned you're my favourite sister in the whole wide world?"

Maeve had already begun opening Cal's half emptied suitcases and popping them on the bed to begin.

"I'm your only sister. That we know of, anyway," Maeve said with a hint of a grin.

"Well, maybe the others won't judge me for my lack of packing skills," Cal joked.

She hopped in for a quick shower to wake her up a little more before venturing out in search of food. Hopefully breakfast and coffee paired with the painkillers she had just taken would shift the fuzziness from her brain. She would probably have to make peace with the dark cloud remaining, though.

"Hey stranger. You've still got a batch of cookie dough left in the fridge. Do you want to use it up after breakfast before we clear out the kitchen?"

Cal glanced up from the plate she was adding food to and smiled at Ray. They had built a nice rapport over their time working in the kitchens this summer and Cal would be sad to say goodbye.

"I'll pop them in the oven once I finish up here. You can take some home to remember me by," Cal replied with a smile.

"You could let me in on the recipe and I'll never forget you," Ray replied with a hint of pleading.

"No can do. You'll have to make do with mediocre cookies until we meet again."

Ray mock pouted before he squeezed Cal's arm lightly and headed back to refill the breakfast pans.

"You *made* them?"

Cal startled and turned toward Haley, who had materialized beside her. Cal's heart beat frantically at their closeness and she sucked in a breath to stop herself from reflexively reaching out to Haley.

"What?" Cal asked as she gathered herself.

She had assumed Haley would avoid her, or at most awkwardly wave at her from a distance. Cal hadn't been prepared for them to be speaking again so soon.

"The cookies. You baked them? Like, from scratch?"

Cal caught up with the conversation and tried to play it off.

"You weren't supposed to hear that. There goes the mystery."

Haley shook her head in disbelief.

"Is there anything you're not good at? Dancing, baking amazing cookies—it's getting a bit ridiculous."

Relationships, for one.

"There's plenty I'm not good at. But the cookies are a point of pride. I should have enough for you to take some with you. I'll give them to you after the show."

"To remember you by?" Haley half smiled as she mimicked Cal's words from her conversation with Ray.

"At least it'll be something good I'm leaving you with," Cal said softly.

Haley studied her face for a moment before she picked up the plate in front of her.

"You've left me with plenty of good, Cal. See you later."

Haley busied herself with filling the plate and Cal understood the conversation was finished. But Cal wasn't ready to let go, not yet. "Are you excited to dance later? Maeve has told my mom all about you changing the dance for her so she can still be in the show. Thank you for that."

Haley paused for a moment, and Cal wondered if she was annoyed that Cal hadn't taken the hint.

"I won't be dancing. But hopefully your mom will enjoy the show. Maeve has been great with the new choreography."

Cal frowned and decided to push her luck while Haley had yet to flee.

"Why won't you be dancing?"

Haley had been so excited about the dance, and Cal knew how much work had gone into it. Cal hoped that missing their last rehearsal wasn't the cause of this, but Haley was more than ready. Truth be told, she had been ready since their first rehearsal together, but Cal hadn't wanted to say that and miss the chance to dance with her all those times.

"Jace's ankle isn't up for it. Wasn't meant to be. I'm going to eat quickly and head over to get set up."

Haley pointed with her thumb toward the gym and walked away before Cal could try to draw out their conversation any longer.

Cal's heart ached for so many reasons where Haley was concerned, but right now mostly for the sadness in Haley's eyes about the dance she wouldn't get to perform. Cal hated the idea of Haley ending the camp with the loss of something that had made her so happy the past few weeks.

The irony of the thought wasn't lost on Cal as she ate her breakfast quickly before making her way to the kitchen to throw on the cookies. If nothing else, she would ensure Haley left with something sweet to remember the summer by.

❖

"Let's get your bags into the car and then you can tell me all the gossip."

Cal began to lift her bag into the boot of the car at her mom's suggestion. She was still lost in her own thoughts, as she had been most of the morning, so the prompting helped push her along.

"You okay?" Clara asked as she shut the boot and turned to Cal.

Apparently, her mood hadn't gone unnoticed by her mom, which Cal couldn't help being thankful for. She wouldn't take for granted being noticed by her mother, even if she'd rather not talk about it.

"She's moody and distant because she screwed things up with Miss Tyne," Maeve piped up to Cal's annoyance.

She didn't even have it in her to admonish her sister, though. It was the truth.

"Oh no. What happened? I was sure that was going somewhere when I visited."

Cal exhaled as the deep ache in her chest made itself known. Not that it had budged much anyway. How did she explain something to her mom that she couldn't describe without delving into what led her here in the first place?

Gee, Mom, what happened is that my childhood was defined by the fallout of your failed relationships, and I don't want the same for Maeve.

"It's not the right time for me to be in a relationship," Cal said. A partial truth was better than a lie.

"So when is the right time?" Maeve asked as they made their way across the car park and through the courtyard.

Each of the kids had a display in the main building with different things they'd done at camp, so they had a plan to go check that out before they needed to get ready for the show.

"When things are a bit more settled."

Cal was grateful that the courtyard was quieter than usual, with most people off showing their displays or packing up. She was conscious that there were far too many ears around to really get in depth about anything.

"You keep saying these things as if they explain anything, and they don't. What's going to make anything more settled than it is right now? Do you even know the real answer, or do you just not want to tell me?"

Maeve sounded frustrated, and Cal bit back her initial equally frustrated retort. She wanted to tell Maeve that it was none of her business, and that she wasn't going to get it. How could she describe the feeling inside her that made it hard not to think that one tiny step toward her own future would throw the balance of their present up in the air once more?

"Let's grab that bench over there, maybe, and have a chat before we go into the building. It looks a bit busy in there," Clara said.

Cal glanced at her mom and nodded at the suggestion. She didn't want to talk, she didn't want to sit down and find ways to explain things that protected her sister's and her mother's feelings. But she was also keenly aware that a room full of people wouldn't stop Maeve from prodding for the truth if she felt it important enough to uncover. By the look on her sister's face, it was obvious that she wasn't letting this go.

"Okay, I'm going to say some things now, and I want you both to listen to me," said Clara.

Cal slid onto the bench across from Maeve as her mom sat beside her. She had assumed it would be her turn to talk when they sat, but she was more than happy to give her mom the floor. She could be the one to tell Maeve that this stuff was complicated and leave Cal to wallow in peace.

"Maeve, I think what Cal is trying to say in a roundabout way is that she doesn't want to get into a relationship because she feels that it's her responsibility to take care of us, and she is afraid to lose her focus on that."

Cal's head snapped up and she opened her mouth to interject, but her mom held a hand up.

"You can tell me how I'm wrong when I'm done, but listen first, okay?"

Cal gulped and nodded. It wasn't that she thought her mom was completely unaware of how Cal felt, but she never expected her to hit the nail so cleanly on the head.

"I've allowed that to happen. I let you take on the responsibility of caring for your sister and for me over the past couple of years while I worked on myself, and even before that. I wish I could change that, Cal, but I can't. I've spent a lot of time in therapy working through the shame that brings me, and I'm finally in a place to address it with you both."

Cal wanted to grab the words and shove them all back inside. She wanted to stop this conversation from unravelling because it was the beginning of so many other ones that Cal wasn't prepared for. She also wanted to protect Maeve from carrying any of this burden, one Cal had had to carry far too young.

"You did your best, Mom. We can talk about this at home, okay?"

Cal reached a hand out and squeezed her mom's gently, to reassure her it was okay. It would all be okay. They could pack this away again and go about their day, and Cal wouldn't hold it against her.

"You always want to talk about things later, but later doesn't happen, Cal. Let Mom talk."

Maeve didn't look angry, but the words still hurt. Cal was trying to protect her, and she didn't understand that.

"I will let Mom talk, but you don't need to hear this right now. It's the last day of camp."

"Stop!"

Cal sat back in shock. Maeve had never raised her voice to her like that, or to anyone, for that matter.

"Stop babying me. You don't think I know the things you don't want me to hear anyway? You not talking about stuff doesn't mean I don't know about it, Cal. It just means I don't have *you* to talk it through with."

"I'm trying to protect you, little May. It's my job."

Cal's throat ached with all of the unsaid words scrambling to the surface. It was the middle of the day, and she was sitting on a bench at a summer camp. It was not the damn time to process this, and she should not be the bad guy for saying so.

"Your job is to be my sister, Kay. That's why I loved this camp so much. Because you stopped babying me and you started treating me like your sister. I already have a mom. I need my big sister."

"You have a mom *because* I protected you. I didn't get that."

The words were out before Cal could stop them, and she clamped a hand over her mouth. She held her breath and waited for the other shoe to drop. For the impact of her words to land square in her mother's chest and be the first chip in the inevitable crack.

"Nobody protected you. And you're still trying to make sure that history doesn't repeat itself with your sister. But I'm here now, Cal. I know you're afraid to see it, but I am not going anywhere. I am here to be Maeve's mom, and I want to work on being yours again too, if you'll let me."

Cal choked on a sob, and arms enclosed around her as she pulled air into her lungs slowly and steadily.

"I'm here, my baby."

Cal gave up on holding them back and let her tears fall against her mom's jacket as she allowed herself to be held in a way she hadn't in far too long.

"I don't want to sound like I'm making excuses, because none of this excuses what you had to go through, Cal. But I've spent a lot of time understanding the generational trauma that's worked its way through our family for so long. The things from my childhood that kept repeating, and the same for my parents before me. They passed their shit down to me, and I passed it to you, and it has to stop here. Three of us right here together, we can stop it. I don't expect you to forgive me for everything right now. I want us to get help to work through the hard stuff together, as a family."

"Like therapy?" Maeve asked as Cal pulled back.

"Yep. Family therapy is all the rage these days, I hear."

"Who needs therapy when you've got a bench in the middle of a camp full of teenagers," Cal joked as she wiped at her eyes.

"I'd like to point out that this could've all been avoided if you just answered me in the first place about Miss Tyne."

Cal glared at Maeve as their mom chuckled and covered both of their hands with hers.

"Your sister is not wrong there. There is so much that I need to make up for with you, and some things I'll never have the chance to. But you missing out on someone who looks at you like you hung the moon cannot be one of them, Cal."

All of this was a lot to take in, but Cal did feel lighter than she had in a long time. The ground was steadier than it had been hours earlier, and the things her mom said weren't empty promises or guilt laden apologies. Her mom spoke with a strength and calmness that Cal understood wasn't new today. It was the first time in a while that Cal was able to hear it, though, and to allow herself to believe it.

"You look at her the same way too. Another reason why I loved this camp so much is because I saw you happier than I ever have before. You love her, don't you?" Maeve asked.

Cal looked at Maeve and saw the truth reflected right back at her.

"It's too late. I've already messed Haley around enough, and she deserves better. She deserves someone who—"

"Who organizes special birthday picnics in the woods and spends hours hanging lights and decorations? Who secretly bakes her triple chocolate chip cookies because it makes her smile? Who spends hours rehearsing a dance with her because you knew how much it meant to her to perform it?" Maeve counted on each finger as she rattled off a list that included things Cal hadn't even known she knew about. "I know I'm the little sister, but that doesn't mean I don't get to give any advice. You may be frustrating and confusing, but you're also the best person I know, and Miss Tyne deserves the best. Don't you think?"

Chapter Twenty-seven

Haley's stomach flipped with nerves and excitement as she stood side stage and watched the groups perform. It wasn't perfect by any means, but that's what made it so wonderfully beautiful. The kids lit up the stage in a way that had Haley beaming with pride. Not at the dance moves, not even when they hit the beat just how they had practiced. Her pride was at the confidence and comfort that shone from each and every one of them. That was the true marker of a job done well.

"They look amazing out there."

Haley's spine tingled at the voice whispering beside her.

Cal.

She hated the way her traitorous body still responded as if it was within her rights to do so. As if Cal's whispered words were to initiate an intimate exchange.

"They do. Shouldn't you be out there watching? Maeve is up soon and again for the grand finale."

Haley glanced at Cal as the kids skipped off giggling and high fiving. It was interval time now as the crew set up for the second half of the show.

"My mom is videoing it all. You should see her, she's like one of those stage parents with her setup." Cal chuckled lightly.

Haley turned a little more to Cal and took in the mix of emotions on her face.

"That must be hard for you," Haley said softly. She didn't

intend to overstep, but she had a feeling that Cal wouldn't allow herself to acknowledge it otherwise.

"It is. But I'm hoping it'll be sort of healing too."

Haley had to hold herself back from reaching out to Cal. That wasn't her place anymore, even if Cal was the one who kept dragging her into conversation. Haley suspected that it was Cal's way of trying to make sure there were no hard feelings, but everything about it was hard.

"What's going on, Cal? Are you trying to be friends?"

Haley hadn't intended for it to sound quite as harsh as it did, but not coming right out and saying what she was thinking hadn't helped things before.

"No, that's not what I want," Cal said.

Haley was surprised to find that a broken heart could still sink. She didn't even know if she wanted to be friends with Cal, if that was even a realistic expectation of herself. But she damn sure didn't want Cal to not want it.

"Then what are you doing here? Because I've tried to be understanding. I know I told you no promises, and you didn't owe me anything. I have no right to be heartbroken, but guess what? I am. So if you don't want to be my friend, what the hell do you want?"

Cal's eyes widened and she glanced around, which reminded Haley of the fact that they were very much not alone.

"Can we go talk over there before the show starts back up, please?"

Haley wanted to refuse, to say no. She had no reason to follow Cal anywhere, but her feet did so without her permission anyway.

"You're wrong," Cal said quietly as they stood inside the small dressing area off to the side of the hustle and bustle backstage.

"Oh gee, thanks for coming all the way here to tell me that," Haley huffed.

Cal bit back a smile as Haley glared at her.

"You keep saying I don't owe you anything as if this was a contract we both signed. But neither of us knew what we were signing up for, Haley. It was all well and good to say no promises when I had no idea I was going to fall in love with you."

"You—wait, what?"

Haley ran through the sentence again in her head. Surely she had misheard, right? Despite her current anger, she knew Cal wasn't heartless enough to declare her love as a parting shot.

"I owe so much more to you than you know. You made me open up in ways I've never done, Haley. You made me face things I've hidden for so long and see myself in a whole new light. The way you see me is terrifying, because I don't think anyone has ever seen the truth of me the way you do. You scare the shit out of me, Trouble."

Cal half grinned at that, but her hands were shaking. She was nervous, and Haley found it annoyingly adorable.

"I'm not that scary," Haley said.

"You definitely are. I've been saying that I can't be in a relationship because I have responsibilities. Because I don't want to lose focus. Because of the way I've seen relationships go in the past and all the destruction they caused. And all of that plays a part, but I know now that I need to stop blaming my past and my mom for not facing my own fears. Truth is, I am terrified that I don't deserve to be loved the way I know you would love me."

Haley reached out and wiped the tear that made its way down Cal's cheek.

"Do. The way I *do* love you. Because newsflash, Cal, you don't actually get to decide whether I do or not. But by denying yourself what you think you don't deserve, you're deciding what *I* deserve, too."

Haley searched Cal's eyes and waited for more. As much as Haley wanted to be the one to decide what she deserved, she also knew she deserved someone who felt the same.

"I'm beginning to understand that. I can't promise everything is better now. I have so much to work on, with my family and myself. But I do know that I feel better when I'm with you. I know that I have this need to do things to make you happy. To make you smile.

And not because I feel like it's my responsibility. For once in my life, I don't feel like I have to do things for you because you need me to. You are the most amazing, capable, brilliant woman I have ever met. You don't need me, I know that. But I sure as hell hope you still want me, Haley Tyne. Because I love you."

Haley had no words to say to encompass everything in her head, so instead she threw her hands around Cal's neck and leaned up to capture her mouth in a kiss. Distantly, she registered the bell dinging to indicate the show was about to return, but she wanted to get lost in Cal's lips and never come back down to earth.

"Is that a yes?" Cal asked as she pulled back.

"Maybe. Depends on what the question is, because you didn't actually ask one."

Cal chuckled and Haley almost melted as Cal's hand slid around her waist to hold her tighter.

"Will you forgive me for being an asshole and be my girlfriend, Trouble?"

Haley tugged Cal down toward her and whispered softly in her ear.

"Before I answer, did you bring the cookies?"

Haley squealed as Cal tickled her lightly and covered her mouth as the first notes of the show started back up again.

"Cookies are for after the show. First, we have something important to attend to."

Haley pouted as Cal pulled back and pointed toward the costume rack.

"You need to change."

Haley frowned in confusion as Cal pulled the hoodie she was wearing over her head and stood with a sheepish smile on her face. She was wearing a plain black shirt, and Haley only then noticed her black pants and shoes.

"Time to pull Baby out of her corner and onto the stage where she belongs. Will you do me the honour of dancing with me?"

Haley gaped at Cal as she caught up to what she was offering to do and then flung her arms around her shoulders again.

"Are you sure? You'd do this for me?"

Cal held her tightly before she pulled back enough to place a featherlight kiss on her lips.

"I'd do just about anything for you, Trouble. But this isn't only for you. I deserve the chance to get back on that stage again and have my mom cheering for me in the crowd. And there is no one I'd rather face this fear with than you. Knowing that at the end of it all I'll have you in my arms helps me remember that it's exactly where I want to be."

Haley had never understood what swooning meant when she read it in books, but she was certain it was exactly what she was doing right now.

"You need to stop saying things like that if you expect me to be able to dance anytime soon."

Cal laughed and kissed her forehead gently. She turned to take the hanger off the rack that held the pink dress Haley had resigned herself to not wearing.

"Get changed and I'll meet you out there."

Haley took the dress and watched Cal walk away as she wondered how in less than fifteen minutes, all of her dreams had come true.

The music softened around them, and Haley's heart thumped from exertion and nerves. This was it, the part they had practiced over and over, the pinnacle of the dance. Haley rarely faltered when it came to performing, but they hadn't rehearsed this in over a week, and this lift was a feat even for the most seasoned of partners.

Haley faced Cal as the music swelled, and the anxiety disappeared in an instant. Cal stood sure, calm, and ready to catch Haley as she leapt. Haley had never been so certain that she would not let her fall. She ran, leapt, and smiled widely as her hips made contact with Cal's firm grip. Haley laughed as the crowd whistled and applauded around them as Cal placed her back on her feet. They were joined by the kids in the makeshift aisle between seats as they danced their way back onto the stage for the end of the song. Haley and Cal took their bows and exited the stage to leave the kids in the spotlight for the grand finale.

"That was amazing." Haley laughed as Cal pulled her into a tight hug.

Adrenaline coursed through them both, and Haley knew her smile was as big as Cal's.

"You are amazing," Cal said.

From anyone else, it would've sounded like a cheesy line. Something Haley would usually scoff at or wave away. But the way Cal said it as she looked at Haley with eyes full of adoration made it sound like the truest words she had ever spoken.

"Is this real? It feels like a dream."

Haley was close to pinching herself as she stood so close to Cal and listened to the final notes of the last song ring out. The audience were applauding, no doubt on their feet, and Haley was full to the brim with emotion. Pride for what all of the kids had accomplished, gratitude for the chance to be a part of it all, love for the woman staring at her in awe.

"It's real. I promise. And don't you dare say no promises, because I plan to make and keep a lot of them. Including delivering the cookies that are hiding in my bag in the changing room."

Haley darted toward the room as Cal laughed and followed behind her.

"Which bag?"

Cal grabbed it and held it behind her back as Haley made to grab it.

"There are cookies in here, but I just wanted to get you alone for a minute before we're invaded by teenagers."

All thoughts of cookies disappeared as Cal slipped a hand behind Haley's back and pressed their lips together. There was a hunger that Haley had missed, and it sent shockwaves through her body.

"Fuck. This was a bad idea," Cal murmured as Haley nipped at her bottom lip. "We have no time to finish this, but I couldn't wait."

Haley pressed her body against Cal's and cursed the fact that they had already emptied their rooms and handed back the keys.

"Do you have work tomorrow?" Cal asked between kisses.

"No. I'm not back till next week. You?"

Haley pulled back as Cal shook her head. Cal's pupils were dark with desire and Haley needed her sooner rather than later.

"There's a hotel not too far from here that we stayed in after Maeve's hospital trip. It's not five stars but it's not bad. Stay with me tonight?"

Haley wouldn't care if it was a tent in the woods at this point, she wanted to be with Cal no matter where it was.

"What about Maeve? I assume they are driving back this evening?"

Cal gulped before she reached out a hand and stroked Haley's face softly.

"They are. If you'll be kind enough to let me tag along, we can road trip home together tomorrow. My mom drove up, so Maeve can go home with her."

Haley wanted nothing more than to follow her body's lead and say hell yes, but she also needed to know it wasn't too much, too soon for Cal.

"You don't need to prove anything to me, Cal. It's okay if you want to take this one step at a time. I don't expect you to drop everything for me, especially where Maeve's concerned. If you need to make sure she gets home safe, that's okay. I'll still want to be with you."

Cal smiled softly and leaned in to kiss Haley again.

"Maeve can text me when she's home. My mom deserves a chance too, and I deserve to spend the night with my beautiful girlfriend. I love my family, and I will always be there for them. But I need to live my life now too, and I want to start doing that tonight. With you."

Haley had been so certain that the end of the show, the camp, the summer would leave her longing for the things she would leave behind as she returned to life as she had always known it. Instead she understood now that life, like this summer, was full to the brim of possibilities waiting for her to embrace them. Something that Haley planned to do wholeheartedly, starting with tonight.

About the Author

J.J. Hale has been devouring books since she was able to hold one and has dreamt about publishing romance novels with queer leading ladies since she discovered such a thing existed, in her late teens.

The last few years have been filled with embracing and understanding her neurodiversity which has expanded the dream to include representing kick-ass queer, neurodivergent women who find their happily ever afters. That dream became a reality with her now two-time Goldie Award–winning debut novel.

Jess lives in the south of Ireland, and when she's not daydreaming, she works in technology, plays with LEGO, and (according to the kids) fixes things.

Books Available From Bold Strokes Books

The First Kiss by Patricia Evans. As the intrigue surrounding her latest case spins dangerously out of control, military police detective Parker Haven must choose between her career and the woman she's falling in love with. (978-1-63679-775-5)

Language Lessons by Sage Donnell. Grace and Lenka never expected to fall in love. Is home really where the heart is if it means giving up your dreams? (978-1-63679-725-0)

New Horizons by Shia Woods. When Quinn Collins meets Alex Anders, Horizon Theater's enigmatic managing director, a passionate connection ignites, but amidst the complex backdrop of theater politics, their budding romance faces a formidable challenge. (978-1-63679-683-3)

Scrambled: A Tuesday Night Book Club Mystery by Jaime Maddox. Avery Hutchins makes a discovery about her father's death that will force her to face an impossible choice between doing what is right and finally finding a way to regain a part of herself she had lost. (978-1-63679-703-8)

Stolen Hearts by Michele Castleman. Finding the thief who stole a precious heirloom will become Ella's first move in a dangerous game of wits that exposes family secrets and could lead to her family's financial ruin. (978-1-63679-733-5)

Synchronicity by J.J. Hale. Dance, destiny, and undeniable passion collide at a summer camp as Haley and Cal navigate a love story that intertwines past scars with present desires. (978-1-63679-677-2)

Wild Fire by Radclyffe & Julie Cannon. When Olivia returns to the Red Sky Ranch, Riley's carefully crafted safe world goes up in flames. Can they take a risk and cross the fire line to find love? (978-1-63679-727-4)

Writ of Love by Cassidy Crane. Kelly and Jillian struggle to navigate the ruthless battleground of Big Law, grappling with desire, ambition, and the thin line between success and surrender. (978-1-63679-738-0)

Back to Belfast by Emma L. McGeown. Two colleagues are asked to trade jobs. Claire moves to Vancouver and Stacie moves to Belfast, and though they've never met in person, they can't seem to escape a growing attraction from afar. (978-1-63679-731-1)

The Breakdown by Ronica Black. Vaughn and Natalie have chemistry, but the outside world keeps knocking at the door, threatening more trouble, making the love and the life they want together impossible. (978-1-63679-675-8)

The Curse by Alexandra Riley. Can Diana Dillon and her daughter, Ryder, survive the cursed farm with the help of Deputy Mel Defoe? Or will the land choose them to be the next victims? (978-1-63679-611-6)

Exposure by Nicole Disney & Kimberly Cooper Griffin. For photographer Jax Bailey and delivery driver Trace Logan, keeping it casual is a matter of perspective. (978-1-63679-697-0)

Hunt of Her Own by Elena Abbott. Finding forever won't be easy, but together Danaan's and Ashly's paths lead back to the supernatural sanctuary of Terabend. (978-1-63679-685-7)

Perfect by Kris Bryant. They say opposites attract, but Alix and Marianna have totally different dreams. No Hollywood love story is perfect, right? (978-1-63679-601-7)

Royal Expectations by Jenny Frame. When childhood sweethearts Princess Teddy Buckingham and Summer Fisher reunite, their feelings resurface and so does the public scrutiny that tore them apart. (978-1-63679-591-1)

Shadow Rider by Gina L. Dartt. In the Shadows, one can easily find death, but can Shay and Keagan find love as they fight to save the Five Nations? (978-1-63679-691-8)

Tribute by L.M. Rose. To save her people, Fiona will be the tribute in a treaty marriage to the Tipruii princess, Simaala, and spend the rest of her days on the other side of the wall between their races. (978-1-63679-693-2)

Wild Wales by Patricia Evans. When Finn and Aisling fall in love, they must decide whether to return to the safety of the lives they had, or take a chance on wild love in windswept Wales. (978-1-63679-771-7)